DISPLAY

REA

ALLEN COUNTY PUBLIC LIBRARY

3 1833 03541 3399

LOVELESS BARKED, "SHOOT THEM BOTH! WE'LL SORT IT OUT LATER!"

Munitia, manning a sort of swivel cannon, took a steady bead on Grant and Gordon and began to squeeze the trigger.

A stream of sticky white synthetic spider silk shot out of the barrel of Munitia's cannon, enveloping both Grant and Gordon. Grant had just time enough to turn to Gordon and say, "Getting caught in a giant spider's web is a part of your plan, right?"

Munitia shut off the web cannon and threw a switch. A small winch began to turn, taking in the silk and hoisting Grant and Gordon off the ground . . .

BLAM! A bullet split the silken cord and dropped the two men roughly but safely back to earth.

"*Where did that come from?*" Loveless demanded. He twisted helplessly in his chair, trying to see something. "Can anyone—?"

"There, sir," a henchwoman said, pointing. "On the port quarter leg. It's—" Her jaw dropped.

"Gott in Himmel! It's West!" Loveless flushed red with outrage.

And then a fair approximation ~~of~~ ~~bullet~~ ~~se.~~

D1176818

ATTENTION: SCHOOLS AND CORPORATIONS

WARNER books are available at quantity discounts with bulk purchase for educational, business, or sales promotional use. For information, please write to: SPECIAL SALES DEPARTMENT, WARNER BOOKS, 1271 AVENUE OF THE AMERICAS, NEW YORK, N.Y. 10020

WILD WILD WEST

STORY BY JIM THOMAS & JOHN THOMAS
SCREENPLAY BY S. S. WILSON & BRENT MADDOCK
AND JEFFREY PRICE & PETER S. SEAMAN

NOVELIZATION BY BRUCE BETHKE

ASPECT®

WARNER BOOKS

A Time Warner Company

If you purchase this book without a cover you should be aware that this book may have been stolen property and reported as "unsold and destroyed" to the publisher. In such case neither the author nor the publisher has received any payment for this "stripped book."

WARNER BOOKS EDITION

Copyright © 1999 by Warner Books, Inc.
All rights reserved.

Aspect® is a registered trademark of Warner Books, Inc.

Front cover movie art by Warner Bros. © 1999 by Warner Bros.
Book design by Charles Sutherland

Warner Books, Inc.
1271 Avenue of the Americas
New York, N.Y. 10020

Visit our Web site at
www.warnerbooks.com

 A Time Warner Company

Printed in the United States of America

First Paperback Printing: July 1999

10 9 8 7 6 5 4 3 2 1

WILD WILD WEST

PROLOGUE

The Civil War swept across the American South like a devastating flood. Wherever it flowed, it leveled towns and factories, uprooted farms and families, and left little but wreckage and national cemeteries in its wake. And in 1865, when the raging waters of war finally began to recede, like a flood, they left detritus washed up in the strangest of places.

In New Haven, Connecticut, a salesman named Oliver Winchester found himself running the Volcanic-Henry Rifle Company, and slowly began to realize that he really did not like that name. In Virginia City, Nevada, a Confederate deserter named Samuel Clemens discovered that he had a certain knack for telling stories, and an urgent need for an anonymous pen name. And in Muhlenberg County, West Virginia, the human flotsam still swirled and churned, like greasy wastewater trying to slide down a half-plugged drainpipe.

In 1861, Virginia had seceded from the Union and joined the Confederacy. In 1863, West Virginia had seceded from Virginia, and rejoined the Union.

In 1869, Muhlenberg County would have seceded from *everybody*, if there'd been anywhere else left to go.

CHAPTER ONE

THE EMPTY FREIGHT WAGON THUNDERED THROUGH A night as black as a mortgage banker's heart. The teamster was drenched with sweat, and nervous as a cat in a room full of rocking chairs. The night was hot and muggy, these mountainous Appalachian roads could be treacherous even in broad daylight, and his horses were dangerously close to the point of total exhaustion. To make matters worse, the two ex-Rebs riding with him kept their lookout far too sharp, and their hands much too close to their Navy Colts, to be actual patent medicine drummers, and they hadn't said more than six words out loud since they'd taken the fork in Sulphur Springs.

Whatever it was they *really* were on their way to pick up, it had to be illegal as all hell. They'd offered the teamster way too much money for an honest day's work, and the way they'd changed their plans when they hit the Huttonsville Road—and their grim insistence on pushing on, even when it was clear that the night was too dark for safe travel—was starting to make him wonder. Maybe his payoff wasn't going to be twenty Yankee dollars in gold in his pocket. Maybe it was going to be two ounces of Rebel lead in his back.

Who the blazes are *these men?* he wondered once again. *Moonshiners?* That almost made a kind of sense. His team and his wagon were made for that kind of work, and it wouldn't be the first time. But the way the two Rebs kept caressing their Colts was not reassuring.

Here in Muhlenberg County, nobody got *that* anxious about running a load of 'shine.

The water in the tank tower was cool and relaxing. The woman, naked and exquisitely beautiful. The cigar?

Captain James T. West, 9th Negro Cavalry, U.S. Army, leaned back, closed his eyes, and took another draw on the hand-rolled ten-cent Virginia Premium Panatela Supremo. He let the thick and bitter smoke roll across his tongue and palate. He listened to what his nose and taste buds were telling him.

They were saying, *Ditch this dogweed and pay attention to the woman.*

West slowly exhaled and decided to take that advice. Now, there'd been a sponge, floating around in here somewhere. He clamped the cigar between his teeth, leaned forward, and began groping through the dark water with both hands. *There, got it.*

The woman let out a startled little squeak and jumped a good six inches straight up. *Oops, maybe not.*

Then she giggled, handed him the real sponge (which she'd been holding all along), and smiled over her shoulder at him as she presented her back for attention. West got that message, loud and clear, and began a long, slow, downward stroke with the sponge that started at the nape of her neck and ended—well, he'd just consider his hands to be off on a little recon mission.

Words began to seem necessary. Damned if he could remember the woman's name, though. Mariah, Melissa; something from the M group, definitely. West opted for a vague pleasantry instead.

"Mighty sweet of you to come along with me while I'm working," he said.

"If this is what you call *work*, Jim West, you sure got a real nice—" She squealed and jumped again.

Okay, and that's how far I can go with the sponge.

"—job," she completed, when his hands had beat a strategic retreat.

West leaned back again and tried another puff on the cigar. It seemed to taste better this time, or perhaps his tongue was simply burning out. "Well, darlin', as I told General Sherman, war is hell."

She frowned. "The war is *over*, Jim honey. It's been over for,"—she paused, straining at the mental arithmetic, eventually doing the subtraction on her fingers—"four years?"

"Not according to the men I'm after."

She shook her head. "Oh, they're just Southern-fried crackers, Jim. Give 'em time; they'll get over it. Why, by the time our kids are old enough to go to school with their kids—"

"*Shh!*" West cut her off with a fast and frightened wave of his hand. "*Company's coming!*" He handed her the sponge and half swam, half bobbed over to the side of the tank. There was a knothole there—a freshly drilled knothole, which anyone would have noticed if they'd decided to refill the tank in the last three days—and West put his ear up to it. "Freight wagon. Empty. Four—no, six horses. They're tired. They've traveled a long way. Moving fast."

The woman sighed, and shook her head in admiration. "Damn, Jim West, you *are* workin'!"

West took his ear away from the knothole just long enough to flash her a charming wink and a cocky smile. "Darlin', I believe that if a thing is worth doin', it's worth doin' well." Then he turned back to the knothole, took the cigar out of his mouth, put his eye up to the hole, and strained to make out detail in the dark. "Ah, there we are." He whistled, soft and low, as the wagon clattered into view. "Well, well, General McGrath's boys. And just when I was about to give up on y'all."

The woman sighed and shook her head again, this time in frustration. *And so another promising evening with Jim West is shot straight to Hell.* West was all business now, ignoring her completely, just as he was ignoring the lit cigar in his own hand. He didn't notice even when she plucked the cigar out from between his fingers and gave the saliva-damp butt end her best long-tongued sensuous lick.

How typical, she thought. She bit down hard on the

cigar, spit out the chunk of tobacco she'd bitten off, then took a deep drag and leaned back against the opposite wall of the tank, to start working up a good sulk.

The empty freight wagon rattled up to the loading dock of an old tobacco warehouse and braked to a sloppy, clumsy stop. The men inside the warehouse had *thug* written all over them—one of them even had it tattooed on the knuckles of his right hand—and he spit out a wad of well-chewed tobacco and greeted the wagon's driver.

"Cletus! Who the sam hell said you *could drive?"*

"I cain't!" Cletus laughed, showing off all the gaps in his rotting teeth.

The thug was annoyed. "You were s'posed to git a wagon and a teamster, you idjit! What happened?"

"Had a little problem with th' teamster," Cletus said. "He done give Billy Ray the evil eye. We had to ask him to git out of th' wagon."

The other Reb on the buckboard seat laughed hoarsely and stroked his Colt. "Yeah. Hadda get out. Heh. On the Parson's Creek Bridge. Splashed *good*. Heh-heh."

The thug on the loading dock frowned, shook his head, and turned around as if looking for something to kick. "Christ, I—well, okay. Can you two useless fools at least back th' wagon up and park it over yonder? And for God's sake, git them horses rubbed down and give 'em some water. They have to live long enough to haul our cargo to New Orleans. You damn near ran 'em to *death*, ya morons!"

Billy Ray dropped off the wagon and wandered into

the warehouse, looking for a bucket, or perhaps a new brain. Cletus nodded and whipped off a ragged salute. "No problem, Corporal!" Then he gave the reins a hard yank, which confused the horses to no end but eventually got the wagon creeping erratically backward.

"And watch out fer that water tower!" Corporal Thug yelled. "That is the single most termite-infested pile of junk I have *ever* seen!"

Candace "Fat Can" Jablonski had every reason to feel proud of herself. She'd never been one for the silly-girl dreams of the other camp followers. Well before Bull Run she'd realized she wasn't the type to land an officer, and that blending in with all the other women who followed General "Fighting Joe" Hooker was never going to give her what she wanted from life. So she'd earnestly worked the oldest profession, saving her money, trading her Jefferson Davis dollars for gold back in early 1863, when everybody else told her she was a fool to do so. Then she'd played the European exchange rates, gone deep on railroad stocks, invested wisely in cattle futures . . .

And now, here she was, eight years later, sole owner and proprietor of the best little whorehouse in West Virginia. She ran a stable of clean and pretty girls, who were just bright enough to know the difference between Yankee and Confederate banknotes (excepting Clarissa, who came from Tennessee and still thought dried tobacco leaves were legal tender). She had a bartender who knew just *exactly* how to cut the whiskey with water and iced tea, so's it wasn't obvious. And just last year, she'd brought in a genuine eye-talian *pianoforte*, imported all the way from Baltimore, and along with it she got that black Joplin kid, who could play it real pretty.

Yes, Fat-Can Candy thought as she surveyed the crowded, smoke-filled saloon, *this is the life, and I'm proud of it.* The men in the room were dirty, drunk, loud, and stinking, true, and half of them couldn't manage to save enough cash money to buy new shoes or a decent suit of clothes—as evidenced by the tattered and thread-bare remnants of Confederate uniforms so many of them still wore—but every last one of them knew they had to pay *her* cold coin on the barrelhead, and on the whole, they were not an unreasonably unpleasant or violent bunch.

Fat-Can Candy smiled to herself, as she turned her hips sideways to pass through the doorway and waddled into the parlor. She was truly a woman who had been there, done that, seen it all, and didn't have a regret or worry in the world.

Excepting Dora.

Candy brought her massive body to a jiggling halt and surreptitiously examined the new girl. It was just as she'd expected, and hoped she wouldn't find. Dora was sitting at the bar—again—studying the men in the room, trying to avoid eye contact with anyone and looking vaguely re-pulsed.

Fat-Can Candy pursed her lips and narrowed her eyes. *Don't tell me I've done it again.*

She *knew* Dora—or rather, Dora's type. She'd seen it

3 1833 03541 3399

a hundred times before, although not so much in the last two or three years. Dora *looked* right. She dressed to kill, like a working girl. She talked the talk, like a working girl. She'd told a truly great story about coming from a high-class bordello in St. Louis when she'd first shown up on Candy's front doorstep, the day before yesterday.

But now that Candy saw Dora in action, she knew she'd done it again. The girl's body language was all wrong. The way she walked, the way she moved her hands; everything was all wrong. The way she couldn't seem to relax enough to really *breathe* was the corker. Dora was clearly not a working girl.

She was a *seeker.*

Fat-Can Candy sighed heavily. She'd taken on a lot of seekers, in her first year or two in business. Sometimes they were trying to find their long-lost husbands, or fiancés. More often they were just dirt-stupid farm girls, looking for that smooth-talking son of a soldier boy who'd marched off to war and left 'em with a belly full of baby and a promise to come back and get married, "later."

Pathetic fools. After the war, by the tens of thousands, Johnny *didn't* come marching home. Because, let's face it: After you've seen the gaslights of Charleston, how are you ever going to go back to pushing a plow and staring at the back end of a mule for the rest of your life?

Candy looked at Dora again and shook her head. It'd been a long time since she'd seen a girl who had it this bad, though. And Dora certainly did look pretty as a five-dollar French girl. So, what the heck. Maybe the situation could be salvaged and even turned to profit. Candy stoked up her resolve, signaled the boiler room to put her legs in forward gear, and set course for the bar.

Dora was staring at a group of men at a table across the room, while trying very hard not to *appear* to be staring. The focus of her attention was a fascinating, motley, and actually somewhat revolting bunch. A few were general-issue thugs, who wore the usual remnants of Confederate uniforms and were in desperate need of shaves and baths. One was a fearsome-looking Indian, with full black warrior braids, incongruously dressed in a Savile Row suit and homburg hat.

But the centerpiece of that tableau: He was a veritable mountain of drunken *pus*. Obese, bearded, and sweating like a Devonshire hog; wearing a greasy and battered enlisted man's kepi and a filthy, stained, Confederate battle jacket that might have fit five years and a hundred pounds ago. Despite the heat he had the jacket buttoned up just as tightly as his rolls of suet would allow, and one of the man's ears had been hacked off—which was not so odd, there were plenty of men missing parts hobbling around these days. But this man wore a strange little brass ear trumpet in its place.

The pile of rancid lard that called itself a man looked up, noticed that Dora was looking at him, and smiled and blew her a grimy kiss. Dora turned away and very nearly blew lunch.

Fat-Can Candy was standing there. "A little rowdier than the top-hat crowd you worked in St. Louis, eh?"

Dora gulped. "They certainly are, Miss Candy."

"Call me Fat-Can. Everyone else does." Candy followed Dora's line of sight to the table across the room, then turned back to Dora. "Your first night out, you may want to stay away from that one. General McGrath has his . . . quirks." Candy raised her arms and took in the room with a flabby, wiggling sweep. "The rest are just lonely boys."

Dora wrinkled her nose. "Lonely . . . *smelly* boys."

"Here." Candy dipped a hand into her monumental jiggling cleavage and came up with a perfume spritzer. "This helps. I know." She gave the perfume to Dora, along with a wink and a friendly smile, then waddled away.

Dora considered the perfume spritzer a moment, then closed her eyes and began squeezing the tiny bulb, in an attempt to erect a barrier of scented fog. While her eyes were closed, something warm, slimy, and disgusting slipped into her ear.

She opened her eyes with a jerk. The jerk had bad teeth, whiskey breath, and eyes that pointed in two different directions at the same time. She was still trying to figure out which eye to look at when he leaned in, tried to lick her ear again, and whispered . . . *something*.

"I'm sorry," Dora said, as her stomach did somersaults. "That won't be possible. I have . . . tonsillitis."

West had seen and heard enough, and his face was starting to hurt from being pressed against the knothole. He backed away, then seemed to realize where he was: still in the water tower, wet and naked, with a woman with a bad case of the pouts. He was mildly surprised that the water around her was not boiling.

West looked at his fingers. "Hmm. Maybe that's enough for me. Gettin' kinda pruney." He tried a charming smile on the woman. "Mind handin' me my clothes?" The smile did not seem to be working. . . .

Corporal Thug and the rest of the gang in the tobacco warehouse were busy loading heavy wooden crates into the wagon. No one had noticed that Cletus had backed the wagon into the base of the water tower, in the process snagging an axle hub on a tower leg strut.

Billy Ray staggered unsteadily out onto the loading dock, carrying a crate all by hisself. "Careful with that!" Corporal Thug hissed. "You want to git us all *killed*? Billy Joe, Bobby Ray, y'all get over there and help—"

"Aw, I can handle it," Billy Ray whined. "See?" He somehow made it over to the wagon and dropped the crate in. It hit the flat wagon bed with a bang.

The horses spooked.

The wagon moved, slightly.

The rotten timbers of the water-tower leg bowed, creaked, and started to splinter. . . .

West enjoyed a good game of keep-away as well as the next boy, but dammit, these were his *pants*, and he was starting to get annoyed with the woman. Then, suddenly, he realized he had an entirely new problem.

There should not be rising surf inside a water tower, he had time to think.

The tower leg snapped.

The water tank tipped precariously.

A massive slosh of water flipped James West out of the tank and carried him crashing down through the glass skylight of the tobacco warehouse, to land miraculously unhurt smack in the middle of Corporal Thug's gang. For a frozen moment the Rebs all just stared at West and stood rooted to their respective spots, wet from the water and slack-jawed with surprise, except for Billy Ray who was slack-jawed even when he wasn't surprised.

West got up, did a quick check for broken bones, and smiled nervously. "Okay, which one of you boys just made a wish?" He pointed at Cletus. "I bet it was you."

Corporal Thug spit some tobacco juice.

West looked up. The woman looked back down at him with wide-eyed raccoon-on-the-railroad-tracks terror. She was still in the sharply tilting water tank; she'd found a handhold and was clutching it with one hand and his clothes with the other.

"I could sure use those clothes about now," West suggested.

She threw his hat down. West caught it, started to put it on his head, then caught himself and used the hat to cover his crotch instead.

Corporal Thug shook the surprise off and took a step forward. "Well, well, looks like we got us a *shy* nig—"

WHAP! West's fist flashed out like a striking rat-

tlesnake, clipping off the rest of the n-word and a good bit
of Corporal Thug's tongue. "I fought four long years with
the Union Army just to never hear that word again," West
snarled. He spun around, to size up the rest of the Rebel
gang. "And you crackers *lost*, remember?" Slowly, cautiously, the Rebs began to move forward and spread out,
to try to encircle West. A few of them picked up axe han-
dles.

One tried a feint from behind. West spun and sent the
man flying with a pivot kick to the head.

"Hey!" He stole a quick glance up at the woman in the
water tower. "How about some *pants*?"

CHAPTER TWO

General McGrath checked his pocket watch again, then impatiently clicked the cover shut and slipped the watch back into his waistcoat. He scowled at Hudson, and his stupid hat. The Indian, as always, was stony-faced and unreadable, and McGrath's scowl went completely wasted. The general let his gaze drift upward to the balcony overlooking the barroom.

Ah, good, the Cass brothers had arrived. They must have come up the back stairs. The older brother, Jack, caught the general's eye, then let him have a brief glimpse of the heavy steamer trunk he and his brother were carrying.

McGrath turned back to Hudson. "I'm still waiting for *my* goods, but I see that my men have arrived with *your* merchandise."

Hudson glanced up, nodded slightly, and said nothing.

McGrath scowled again. "Actually, I was rather expecting to deliver this package personally to Dr.—"

Hudson interrupted. "My employer, here, in a brothel?" The stone face cracked into a small, ironic smile. "That would be quite . . . tautologically superfluous."

McGrath frowned. He wasn't sure what he found more annoying: Hudson's stupid hat; his precise, almost British, diction; or his tendency, on those occasions when he did lower himself to speak, to pepper the conversation with ten-dollar words that General McGrath didn't know.

Hudson spoke again. "You will meet him when the time and place are appropriate. Now, General McGrath"—Hudson stood up—"shall we go upstairs to examine the 'merchandise'?"

McGrath thought it over, then shook his head. "Frankly, Mr. Hudson, I was not planning to walk those oaken stairs with you. Direct me to the poot, sirrah. Something young and creamy. A gamer, that takes to the crop and spur."

"As you wish." Hudson nodded again, slightly, then turned and walked away. McGrath sighed, belched, farted, and took another survey of the available talent in the room.

Dora had made it as far as the foot of the stairs when a grimy hand snaked out from behind a potted palm and grabbed her. It was the cross-eyed drunken jerk, again.

"Y'all drive a hard bargain, lady. All right, *fifty* cents

to take them big juicy lips and ..." He grabbed her cheeks and tried to steer her head down.

"Still *not interested*," she growled through clenched teeth. She tried to pull away. He wouldn't let go.

"But you *gotta* be innerested. You're a *whore*."

Dora pulled away from the jerk's grip and stood up tall. Suddenly, there was fire in her eyes, and ice. Her voice, when it came out, was a baritone growl. *"That doesn't mean a girl can't have high standards."*

And then she coldcocked the jerk.

James West was a fighting man, pure and simple. In three tours with the Union Army he'd learned it all, mostly in bars while on leave, and he'd put it all together in a style that was uniquely his own. From the slums of San Francisco's Chinatown came the hand that went into the sleeve and emerged as a *shakoken* palm-heel strike. From the French Quarter of New Orleans came the swift kick in the *boulés* that dropped the man with the bowie knife like a brain-dead side of beef. And from Wanda Lou Jones's three older brothers came the ability to run, turn, and punch while simultaneously pulling his pants up.

Corporal Thug and his gang never stood a chance.

That didn't stop them from trying, though.

West was nearly dressed now, and starting to get *seriously* annoyed. "Could I have a little privacy here?" he shouted, as he opened a can of whupass on another slow learner. As if in response there came a female shriek from above, and the grinding, splintering sound of the water tower completing its final collapse. West jumped to the side as a thousand gallons of cold water crashed through what remained of the skylight, effectively ending the fight and flushing the rest of Corporal Thug's gang out into the alley.

"Thank you," West said. He looked out the door, saw that the tower had collapsed because the terrified horses had finally pulled the wagon free of the wrecked leg, then looked up, took a slight step to the side, positioned himself just so—

And caught the falling, naked, screaming woman.

"You'll have to excuse me, darlin', but my evidence is gettin' away." West gallantly set the woman on her feet, jumped up to grab an overhead block and tackle, and went sailing through the warehouse, to drop into the back of the runaway wagon at the precise moment as it thundered past the loading dock. Then he stood up in the back of the wagon, turned around, and gave the naked, terrified, shivering woman a gentlemanly tip of his hat.

"Sorry about there not being any towels!"

"**D**ora" knew the secret to making an entrance was timing. She'd hung back, as Candy herded all the available girls together and started parading them past General McGrath. Then she'd watched as McGrath's flabby, pustulant face wobbled through its small range of emotions. Boredom, indifference, impatience . . .

Ah. And *now* was the precise moment to upstage all the other tarts. Dora slowly and casually strolled into view, gave her hips a flirtatious tilt, and began innocently licking a bright red lollipop.

McGrath's rheumy eyes widened. A line of tobacco-colored drool trickled out of the left corner of his mouth. He waved the other girls away, beckoned for Dora to come closer, and cleared his throat.

"Uh, what's your name, little missy?"

"Dora," she said in a small and childish voice. She took another lick on the lollipop. "Would you like to go upstairs?"

McGrath gave a pleased little shudder that made his jowls quiver. "Oh indeedy, I would." He tried to stand; Dora helped him make it to his feet on the second try. McGrath took one lurching, drunken step toward the stairs.

Then stopped.

"But not just yet," McGrath said, leering. He leaned in close to Dora, and put his grimy lips up to her ear. Dora repressed a shudder; the man smelled of sweat, grease, bad whiskey, and way too much time spent around horses without cleaning his boots. "Nothing stokes the fire in my loins," McGrath said, "like . . ."

Dora gulped nervously.

". . . a ditty!"

Dora blinked. "A what?"

"A *song*! C'mon girl! Sing for me!"

Dora shook her head, obviously frightened by the request. "But . . . General. I assure you, my talents really lie elsewhere."

McGrath gave her a hard swat on the rump. "Y'all got some pretty fair lungs on ya, gal. Now use 'em!" He more collapsed than sat in the nearest chair, which groaned under the weight, and the room grew suddenly and terrifyingly quiet. All eyes that were sober enough to focus were on Dora. She looked up. Even the two men on the balcony, the ones with the steamer trunk, were staring down at her.

Trembling, Dora turned and strolled over to the piano, fighting the urge to run screaming from the room. Joplin, the piano player, looked up at her expectantly. " 'Sons of the South'?" Dora whispered. He nodded and struck up the intro.

"*I was innocent, I was pure,*" Dora began, in a hoarse, weak, and badly off-key voice that was barely more than a husky whisper. "*Pure as the fluffy famous driven snow. I thought babies turned up at the door, brought by storks who know just where to go.*

"*As a blossom of the deep, deep South, life was sweeter than a pint of gin. Then those Yankee troops deflowered me, launching me on my life of sin. . .*"

The runaway freight wagon raced through the center of town, drawn by six wild and terrified horses. The lid of the crate Billy Ray had dropped flew off as the wagon slammed across a series of bad ruts, and West fought to keep both his hat and his footing. Then he caught a glimpse of what was inside the crate and very nearly lost his cool.

"*Holy—!*" He did a double take, and looked at the clinking glass vials again. "Cousin-humpin' crackers got a wagonful of *nitroglycerine!*"

West's first impulse was to drop to his knees and try to

steady the clinking glass vials—*No, wait, that's stupid. This whole wagon is a bomb.* Maybe throw the nitro overboard? *Oh, great, blow up the town and scare the scat out of the horses.*

The horses! West jumped to his feet, clambered over the other crates, threw himself into the driver's seat and grabbed for the reins—

No reins. He had a brake handle, but no reins. West could see clearly now; the reins were gone. Some stupid cracker had forgotten to tie them off, and they'd fallen down between the horses and were dragging on the ground. *Damn, that ground is going by fast!* Too fast to jump off and let the horses run themselves out. 'Sides, if he let them run they'd probably dump the wagon, and there was enough nitro in here to flatten the entire town. . . .

West took a breath, steeled his nerves, and jumped onto the left rear horse. *This is stupid.* He somehow managed to get his feet down onto the harness bar without getting himself killed. *This is really, really stupid, Jim.* Balancing on the bar, leaping from horse to horse and grabbing whatever tack his fingers could find, he worked his way forward. *But it ain't any more stupid than that charge at Gettysburg.* His foot slipped; he caught himself and pulled back up. *Reckon it's about Medal of Honor stupid.* Almost there. He reached; stretched fingers out; just two more inches. He lunged for the lead horse's halter—

The horse shied, and West fell.

* * *

Dora had worked some tough rooms before, but this one was a killer. Nothing but table after table of stony, scowling, ugly mugs, all looking like they might start pelting her with beer bottles at any moment.

"*Georgia with your peaches, arise. Virginia with your creepers, arise. Kentucky with your bourbon, Texas with your rangers, Missouri with your compromise—Arise, damn your eyes!*"

And the centerpiece of it all, that ugly pus bag Mc-Grath, was sitting there like some scabrous drunken Buddha—

Wait! What's that? McGrath is starting to tap his foot? He's starting to smile?

Dora tore into the next verse with renewed gusto. "*Down with the North and its Yankee doodle! Don't hang there limp like a soggy noodle!*"

An instant before going under the pounding hooves West caught hold of a dangling chain, and hung on for dear life. The view from this angle wasn't any better though, because now he could see that the linchpin was loose and had just about worked its way out. *Damn! These crackers do not know how to take care of vehicles!*

Hmm. Wonder if I can kick the pin out? Separate the team from the wagon? West discarded the idea almost as soon as he thought of it. *Nah. Wagon flips, nitro blows, town's destroyed, horses drag me to death. Not an option.* Which left—

Straining with every ounce of his strength, West pulled

himself back up onto the topside of the harness bar and
grabbed for the lead horse's halter, this time catching it.

"*Whoa!*"

The horses ignored him and took a hard swerve left.
The wagon careened around the corner on two wheels
and nearly flipped. West grabbed both lead horses by the
ears.

"*I SAID,* WHOA!"

Incredibly, the horses stopped.

Keeping a firm grip on the lead horse's halter, West
jumped down, grabbed the reins, then eased back to the
wagon and set the parking brake. He tied the reins off to
the brake handle, slapped the dust from his clothes,
tch-ed at the scuff marks on his hand-tooled cowboy
boots, then stood up, straightened his hat, and tried to figure out just where the hell he'd ended up.

Just up the hill from a whorehouse, it seemed. Looked
like a classy joint, too. Red lights on the veranda, expensive sign out front saying *Fat Can Candy's*, tinny piano
music sifting through the stale night air. Some horribly
off-key woman was singing, or maybe the yokels inside
were doing something unspeakable to a cat. West was
about to turn his attention back to the wagon when a face
like a rusty fishhook caught his eye. He took a step off to
the side to get a better view, and squinted.

"Well, well," West said softly, "this *is* workin' out to
be my lucky day. General Bloodbath McGrath." Unconsciously, West's fingers curled around the butt of his Colt.

No, the inner voice of his good sense advised him.

There must be thirty Rebs in there, all braying along with that poor god-awful demented screech owl. And you got a warrant for McGrath's arrest, not a license to kill.

West pulled the Colt from his holster, took a quick look to make sure that the barrel wasn't plugged with dirt and that he was ready to bust caps, then reholstered the gun and faded into the darkness, slipping toward the back stairs of the whorehouse.

"*. . . sons of the Southland, rise up! Stiffen your guts and rise up! Be firm, be fearless, be erect; Sons of the South, arise!*" Dora finished the song to rousing, drunken applause and twirled into a curtsy. McGrath jumped to his feet, grabbed Dora's hand, and made a beeline for the stairs. He had to stop to catch his breath at the landing, though, so Dora took the lead as they moved through the upstairs hallway. She opened the first bedroom door—

Ooops. Occupied.

She opened the second bedroom door—

Two Rebs were in there, sitting on a steamer trunk. A third person was in a burlap sack on the floor, wiggling like a caterpillar. Dora giggled. "Well, *that's* a new one."

McGrath slammed the door and dragged Dora into a yet another bedroom. He released her hand as he sat down heavily on the bed and began bouncing up and down, testing the springs. Beckoning for her to come closer, he hiked up his coat and began to unbutton his britches.

Suddenly, Dora seemed strangely shy.

"Don't let the ear scare you," McGrath said. "I lost it at Chickamauga."

Dora blinked. "Oh, really? One can hardly notice." She smiled at McGrath, and began fiddling with her large gold belt buckle. "Would you mind . . . ? It . . . seems to be stuck." She took a step closer.

"Say no more," McGrath said. He reached for the buckle. Before he could touch it, though, it popped open, to reveal a spiraling mesmeric screen.

McGrath was already half-stupefied from the night of drinking. The mesmerizer simply pushed him over the edge. "Wha . . . what's this?" he asked, thickly, unable to take his eyes off the spiraling pattern.

"It's a deep, deep pool," Dora said gently, in a slow and soothing voice. "Maybe it's your old swimming hole. Are you getting sleepy, General?"

McGrath's jowls sagged. "Yes. Sleepy." His knees buckled, and he sagged to the floor.

"Good. You can sleep now."

"Sleep." McGrath's eyelids slowly closed.

"General?"

McGrath snored.

Dora stood up, checked to make sure the door was locked, then took in and blew out a deep breath.

When Dora spoke again, it was with a man's voice.

"Very good. Now, when I snap my fingers, you're going to be my little doggy. And when I say 'speak,' you're going to tell me everything I want to know. Understand?" Dora's fingers snapped.

"Woof!" McGrath said.

Dora nodded, and smiled. "All right, little doggy: sit up."

McGrath sat up. His tongue lolled out. He panted.

"Now, tell me: who's in that sack in the next room? Is it the scientist, Dr. Escobar? Speak!"

"Woof! Woof!" said McGrath.

"No, speak *words*, doggy! Tell me the name of the man you kidnapped him for. Speak!"

McGrath growled and tried to bite Dora's fingers.

"Bad dog! Now, lie down, and watch the swirling spiral!"

There was just one problem.

The spiral had stopped swirling.

McGrath growled again, then blinked. It was a waking-up-after-a-bad-drunk-where-the-hell-am-I-and-who-the-hell-are-you? kind of blink. "Uh-oh," Dora said. She looked down, noticed that the mesmeric spiral had stopped turning, and started frantically fiddling with the gizmo.

West, out on the porch roof, had been watching McGrath and the whore through the closed window. He didn't hear what they said, but the way McGrath *acted* was weird enough. Then, clearly, something went sour. The girl started frantically futzing with her belt buckle, and McGrath turned even meaner and nastier than usual. West shook his head. This might get ugly.

When he saw McGrath draw the boot knife, West went on instinct and dived headfirst through the window.

McGrath was startled, half-drunk, and slow to react.

West came through the glass and the chintz curtains in a tuck and roll, kicked the knife from McGrath's hand, and cold cocked him with the follow-through punch. Then, having gotten a 10.0 on technical, West went for the style points, and bounced to his feet and tipped his hat to the hooker.

"Didn't mean to startle you, ma'am," West said, flashing his trademark cocky smile. "But it looked like you needed some help."

The hooker blinked rapidly, gulped, shook her head, cleared her throat. . . .

"Er, looks can be deceivin', dark stranger."

Yep, West thought, *it's that off-key screech owl from the bar all right. McGrath always was tone-deaf.*

"But I assure you, sir, I am perfectly fine."

"Good." West turned his attention to McGrath's porcine, unconscious form. He quickly patted the man down, removing another knife, a tobacco plug, a Spiller & Burr revolver, and a small, heavy, leather bag.

West checked the bag. Gold coins. He turned to Dora, who was still standing there, looking confused. "A woman like you gets top dollar, I expect." He tossed her the bag. "Here you go. Now, run along. McGrath is mine."

She shook her head. "No, *you* run along. He's *mine.*"

West did not expect this turn of events, and was nonplussed. "Come on, lady, you got the money. Have some dignity."

She stamped her foot. "No, you listen to *me* . . ."

*   *   *

General McGrath thought he was awake, maybe. Either he had a killer hangover, or he'd been in one hell of a barroom brawl, or he was having the worst nightmare of his entire life. He seemed to be lying facedown on a hard wooden floor, with a five-alarm bell-clanging death-defying headache in progress, and two really stubborn people have a really *stupid* argument right over his throbbing head. He got one bleary eye open, then the other, then both open at the same time. . . .

"WEST!"

McGrath came off the floor like a furious grizzly bear and caught West in the small of the back, driving him clean through the shattered wooden door and out into the hallway. A half dozen other doors banged open at the sound of McGrath's roar, and a mob of half-dressed Rebs and screaming women poured into the hall.

Where'd that Indian get that stupid hat? West wondered. Then he caught McGrath with a good solid elbow in someplace that crunched, followed up with a quick heel kick to the *cojones*, and heaved the stinking, roaring monster off him.

BLAM! A pistol shot splintered the wood inches from West's head.

"*NO GUNS!*" McGrath shouted. "*I WANT THIS NIGRA SONUVABITCH ALIVE!*"

Dora took advantage of the confusion to slip out of the room and down the hall. There was a guard by the door to the first bedroom; Dora flashed him a disarming smile, then dropped the man with a lead-weighted sap to the temple. The guard had a revolver. Dora took it and pushed the door open.

Hudson was in there, with his back to the door, barking orders. *"Get Dr. Escobar out of here!"*

Dora cocked the pistol and pressed it against the back of Hudson's neck. "Leave Doctor Escobar right there." Hudson whirled around—

The brawl in the hallway exploded through the door. Dora got knocked flying. Hudson chopped the gun out of Dora's hand, drove a fist right between the mascara lines, and threw her out into the hall. West and Dora collided and tripped over each other, while Hudson and his men scarpered out the back way.

Dora tried to chase Hudson and collided with West again. West tried to shove Dora aside and go after McGrath.

"Look at it this way!" West shouted. "Lose a lop-eared general's business tonight, make it up on a teamster's convention tomorrow! Now get out of my way, lady!" They both tried to move and collided again.

"No!" Dora shouted, every last trace of femininity gone from "her" voice. "I'm no lady, and you get out of *my* way!" He whipped off his wig.

West's Colt flashed into his hand. *"Freeze!* U.S. Army!"

But Dora had both a Colt and a badge. *"You* freeze! U.S. Marshal!"

* * *

There was an expensive black brougham parked next to the freight wagon full of nitroglycerine. A woman sat in the window seat of the carriage, studying the action in the whorehouse with opera glasses. "Freeze, U.S. Army," she said in a flat voice. "You freeze, U.S. Marshal."

"Oh, dear," said the man sitting in shadows. His voice was soft, Southern, and aristocratic.

Hudson and his men raced up the hill to the parked carriage. "Federal agents inside, sir!"

"So Miss Lippenreider informs me." The man sighed. "Still, I believe that good manners dictate we should send out . . . " A long cane telescoped out of the darkness, to poke the linchpin out of the freight wagon and release the parking brake.

". . . the welcome wagon." Slowly at first, then with increasing speed, the wagon full of nitroglycerine began to roll down the hill toward the whorehouse. Hudson and his men threw the scientist-in-a-sack into the carriage next to Miss Lippenreider and climbed aboard. The driver gave the horses a touch of the whip.

Inside Fat Can Candy's, Jim West was confused. Okay, so McGrath's whore was actually a man—which went a long way towards explaining the wretched singing voice—but this man was also a U.S. Marshal. But West's orders came directly from the Secretary of the Army himself, while the marshals' service answered to . . . West had never been terribly clear on this whole military-civilian chain-of-command thing. *Rank* he understood; he didn't respect it, but he understood it. But in this situation, where he was pointing a cocked gun at a man who was waving a U.S. Marshal's badge in his face, who was also supposed to be on the same side . . .

West looked at the marshal. "Okay. Now what?"

. . . and then the wagon full of nitroglycerine hit the back porch of the best little whorehouse in West Virginia, and Jim West found himself flying . .

CHAPTER THREE

The train chugged into Arlington Station and came to a stop with a sigh of steam. James West got to his feet, pulled his saddlebags and silver-handled cane out from under the seat, and limped out of the passenger car and onto the station platform. He'd been intending to catch a hansom cab next, but when he saw the shiny black mustang parked out in front of the livery stable across the street, he *knew* he had to change his plans.

Half an hour later he was dressed for riding, across the Potomac River, and trotting up broad, tree-lined, Pennsylvania Avenue. The rental horse seemed to handle the wagon traffic and clanging streetcars okay, but it was positively spooked by all the people pedaling those new-fangled high-wheeled gizmos—

Velocipedes, West remembered. *Dumb name. They got two wheels. Why not call 'em . . . oh,* bicycles?

West shook his head, let the thought go, and relaxed enough to slip into a brief and pleasant flashback. It'd been years since he'd ridden right smack up the middle of Pennsylvania Avenue; four years, to be exact. He could still remember the date and the occasion: May 24, 1865, the Grand Review of the Union Armies.

It'd been a clear, hot, brilliantly sunny day. General Meade had led the eighty-thousand-man Army of the Potomac in review the day before, marching past the cheering thousands who lined the street from Capitol Hill to the White House, and then on the twenty-fourth it was General Sherman's turn. For six hours, the sixty-five-thousand-man Army of Georgia passed in review before President Andrew Johnson and General in Chief Ulysses Grant. Then, at about three in the afternoon, Lieutenant James West and the 9th Negro Cavalry brought up the rear. *The people of Washington cheered my men like heroes that day.*

A week later Meade's and Sherman's soldiers were discharged and sent back home, Congress was arguing over whether black men should be allowed to own guns and vote, and the 9th Cavalry was riding a slow cattle train bound for North Dakota. Seems the Lakotah Sioux were getting restless again. . . .

West allowed himself a wry smile. *Damn, that was a tough assignment. I sure hope General Custer and the 7th Cavalry have a better time out there than we did.*

He thought of General George Armstrong Custer, hero of the Battle of Appomattox Station, racing back and forth in front of the president's reviewing stand because he'd lost control of his horse, and that brought West back to the here and now. The cheering crowds and reviewing stands were long since gone, of course, but there was still a line of hitching posts in front of the White House main gate. West dismounted—winced a bit as he put weight on his sore leg—then tied the horse off to a post, pulled his cane from the rifle scabbard, and limped up the stairs into the White House.

He spotted the plainclothes guards before the first one got his feet off the desk. Four men; cheap New York suits; bulges in the wrong places, probably Merwin-Hulbert .44s. They moved in to block West, and the guy in charge seemed to be—

Glory be, this is old home week. Allan Pinkerton!

West knew Pinkerton, and didn't think too highly of him. Before the war Pinkerton had been a Chicago cop, then a private detective. After Lincoln got elected the man used his political connections to get himself appointed head of Army Intelligence, and was so bad in the job that he pretty much single-handedly ruined the career of General George McClellan. After the fiasco at Antietam, Lincoln sacked McClellan, demoted Pinkerton to trolling Washington cocktail parties for Confederate spies, and turned Army Intelligence over to Lafayette Baker, who, as far as West was concerned, walked on water.

Which immediately posed three questions. *Who let this fool back into the White House? Does Lafe Baker know he's here?* And, *Do you suppose Allan remembers me?*

Pinkerton stepped forward. "Now hold on there, pardner," he said, sneering. "Mr. Lincoln may have given your kind forty acres and a mule, but you can't just walk into the Oval Office."

No, I'd say Allan doesn't.

Pinkerton nodded at the Colt Army .44 on West's right hip. "Now, hand over that gun, boy."

West smiled. *This is gonna be fun!*

"Oh," West said innocently, "you mean, *this* gun, sir?" He propped his cane against his leg, moved his right hand to cover the grip of the Colt, and began flexing his fingers, as if getting ready for a fast draw. Pinkerton went tense. Behind him, his agents began fumbling for their own weapons. All their eyes were locked on West's right hand.

That's right, gentlemen. Watch the birdie.

West's left-handed draw took them completely by surprise. By the time the agents registered it, the twin barrels of West's 12-gauge Greener "Street Howitzer" were pressed firmly against Pinkerton's crotch.

"Or this one?" West asked.

For a moment, the scene froze, as the inner voice of West's good sense piped up. *Hey Jim, let's hope these guys like Allan more than most people do. Otherwise, one of them might just say "Fair trade" and go for it.* West watched as a bead of sweat broke out on Pinkerton's forehead and trickled down his cheek.

Then a familiar, gravelly voice broke in and ended the standoff. "Captain West! Stop toying with Mr. Pinkerton!" West smiled at Pinkerton and put up the shotgun.

Allan hastily backed away, almost colliding with his own men in the process. "Mister Pinkerton!" President Grant continued. "Do not make Captain West any later than he already is!" The tangle of agents parted like the Red Sea, giving West clear passage to the door of the Oval Office.

West reholstered the shotgun, collected his cane, and smiled. "I gots to go," he said to Pinkerton. "President dude wants to rap wif me. By the way, Rosie O'Neal Greenhow said to say hello." Pinkerton shot West a glare that could have driven ten-penny nails. West merely touched his cane to his hat brim and walked on by.

Once West was inside the Oval Office, President Grant shut the door, then crossed over to his desk and pulled a cigar from the humidor. "Don't be too hard on the Pinkertons, West." He clipped the end off the cigar with a little gizmo that looked like a pocket guillotine. "What with Reconstruction and all, I'm a very popular man these days. Got over a hundred death threats last week alone. Lafe Baker is retired and happy now, and not interested in restarting the Secret Service, so the Cabinet made me hire some damn private detectives." Grant lit the cigar, then seemed to remember his manners. "Drink? Cigar?"

West nodded. "Thank you, sir." West limped across the room to the side table, poured himself two fingers of Kentucky bourbon, and selected a cigar and sniffed the leaf. He turned around to find Grant studying him.

"What the hell happened to your leg?" Grant asked.

West was embarassed. "Just a, er, riding accident, sir."

"You rode a wagonload of nitroglycerine through the roof of a whorehouse, is what *I* heard." West shifted uncomfortably as Grant chuckled. "Also, *I* heard that you let General McGrath get away again."

West's embarrassment instantly flashed into anger. "Sir, I staked out a band of gunrunners on a tip that that cracker son of a . . . that McGrath was going to show. From there, I trailed him to the whorehouse. Then, just when I had him right in my hands, some half-a-sissy marshal wearing a dress ruined—"

Grant nodded. "Artemus Gordon."

West was surprised. Again. "You know him?"

Grant favored West with another scowl. "Captain West, of course I know him. He's the best marshal I've got! Gordon is a genius!"

West blinked, unbelieving.

Grant went on. "Time and again, Gordon has proven himself to be a very cunning operative with a rapacious intellect. *Nothing* will stop him from completing a mission for the president . . ."

Grant slammed a fist down on the desktop.

". . . except the impulsive actions of some headstrong cowboy!"

West looked down at the fist Grant had slammed on the desktop, then calmly drew his Colt and pressed it against Grant's forehead. "Who are you?" he asked.

Grant was livid. "*I am the President of the United States!*"

"Wrong answer." West thumbed back the hammer and fired a shot into the ceiling. Grant jumped a good foot in the air. Bits of lath and plaster rained down. The hallway door burst open, and Pinkerton and his men rushed in, guns drawn.

West was holding his pistol pressed against Grant's temple. "Hi, Allan," West said.

Pinkerton cocked his revolver and took a solid bead on West. "Take that gun away from the President's head! *Now!*"

"Be happy to," West said softly. "Only, this ain't the president." West reached forward, grabbed Grant's right wrist, and held it up so that Pinkerton could get a good look. "This is a Harvard class ring. The president graduated from West Point."

Grant's back stiffened. "See here, West."

West nudged him with his pistol. Grant shut up. "Now," West said to Grant, "let's try this again. Who are you?"

Angrily, Grant straightened his coat. "I *am*—"

West cocked his pistol.

"— Artemus Gordon."

West smiled, lowered his gun, and uncocked it. Allan Pinkerton made a fantastic intellectual leap. "*That man is an imposter!*"

West nodded. "Excellent work, Pinkerton. Now, do you want to shoot him, or shall I?"

"That won't be necessary," Gordon said in a smooth, baritone voice. He carefully raised his hands to his face and began peeling off his fake beard. Pinkerton apparently recognized Gordon and lowered his gun.

A familiar, gravelly voice broke in from off to the side. Again. "*Will somebody please tell me what the hell that stunt was all about?*" West, Gordon, and the Pinkertons turned. President Grant—the *real* President Grant, this time—was standing in another doorway, with his hands on his hips, a cigar in his teeth, and a scowl on his face.

West prodded Gordon in the (now obviously fake) belly with the barrel of his pistol. "Well?"

Sheepishly, Gordon finished peeling off the rest of his facial makeup. "Sir," he said to Grant, "in perilous times like these, I was simply illustrating how someone impersonating you could actually walk right into the very bowels of the White House." While Gordon was talking, West sidled over to the president's desk and found a dagger-shaped letter opener. When Gordon finished talking and turned back to him, West jabbed the letter opener into Gordon's fake gut. The air hissed out of the inflated bladder, finishing with a flatulent *R-R-RIP*. One of the Pinkerton agents covered his mouth and snickered.

President Grant simply glared and shook his head. "You're clever, Gordon. Too clever for your own good. One of these days it's going to get you killed."

West sensed an opportunity to ingratiate himself to Grant and seized it. "Ain't that the truth, sir. Like the other night, he had this little twirly belt buckle thing that was 'sposed to hypnotize McGrath. Only the twirly thing busted, and McGrath just about stuck an Arkansas toothpick up Gordon's petticoats."

Grant didn't so much as crack a smile. Instead, he was looking up at the thin plume of plaster dust trickling down from the bullet hole in the Oval Office ceiling.

When he lowered his gaze, it was to fix West with a disapproving eye.

"On the other hand, West, not every situation calls for your patented approach of shoot first, shoot again, maybe shoot a third time—and then when they're all dead, start thinking about maybe trying to ask a question or two."

Gordon couldn't resist. "Yes, sir. Like diving headfirst through a plate-glass window to rescue little ol' me. *Brilliant* plan. *Très gallant*, yes, but—"

"That's why working together will be good for both of you," Grant continued.

West and Gordon were both stunned. "*What?*" West blurted out. "Sir, I work—"

"The way your commander in chief orders you to work," Grant completed. He turned to address the detective. "Pinkerton, get your men back out into the hallway and hopefully, a little more wide-awake on the job." Grumbling, the Pinkertons left. "West, Gordon? Follow me." Grant wheeled and marched out of the room. Jostling for position, West and Gordon followed.

The president led them through a side door, down a hallway, and up to a set of double doors guarded by a pair of unsmiling and heavily armed Marines in long blue coats and tall belgic caps. "Gentleman?" said Grant, pausing dramatically. "*Welcome to the War Room.*" With a grand sweep, he threw the doors open.

For a few moments even James West, who made it a practice never to be awed by anything, was overwhelmed by the scale and spectacle of the War Room. The room was *huge*, and still it managed to be cluttered with maps, desks, people, and machinery. Military officers in uniform and civilian staff members in suits mixed and conversed in low voices, while clerks and aides scampered back and forth like gophers. Telegraph receivers clattered incessantly, pantographs churned without pause, and in one corner something that appeared to be an offset letterpress spewed forth printed paper in prodigious volumes. Five large maps, showing North America, South America, Europe, and the Atlantic and Pacific Oceans respectively, dominated the walls, while a cadre of staff members stood before the maps, urgently moving colored pins, bits of yarn, and tiny toy ships.

Grant ushered West and Gordon inside, then shut the doors behind them. "West," he said, "you've been pursuing McGrath ever since Appomattox."

Gordon blinked in surprise. "Four years? I found him in two weeks, and I wasn't even looking for him."

West skewered Gordon with a glare but said nothing.

Grant stepped over to a display of photographs on a bulletin board. All the images depicted distinguished, bewhiskered men. "Ten of the country's top scientists have disappeared recently. *Top* people, in metallurgy." He tapped one photo. "Hydraulics." He tapped another. "Explosives." He tapped a third, then turned back to West. "Gordon was on an assignment to find them."

West smirked at Gordon. "Did you check under your dress?"

Grant cleared his throat. West and Gordon behaved like adults for a moment. "The *point*, gentlemen, is that we now know it was McGrath who was doing the kidnapping. You two have been working on the same case all along. Why did it take you so long to realize it?"

"Well, sir," West said, "one of us was still trying to figure out if he was a man or a woman."

Grant sighed and rubbed his temples, as if he was starting to develop a severe headache. He regarded West through narrowed eyes, and apparently decided to give it one more try.

"The South is not accepting Reconstruction gracefully. Now that we know McGrath is involved in the kidnappings, we can be certain that *someone* is trying to raise and equip a new Confederate Army. The men who were kidnapped have knowledge of tremendous military and industrial value."

West interrupted. "Begging your pardon, sir, but that's not McGrath's style. He raids government arsenals and steals guns and ammo."

Grant nodded. "Exactly. Which means *someone else* is the brains behind this operation!"

A military aide strode up smartly, saluted, and handed a telegram to the president. Grant read it and sighed heavily.

"Our nation is still weak from the war, gentlemen. And the vultures are circling." He held up the telegram. "*Spanish warships sighted off the coast of Florida*," he read. He shook his head, then used the piece of paper to gesture across the room at the map of the United States. "*British troops massing on the Canadian border*. Probably still mad about that business with Meagher's Brigade." Grant shook his head again, then pointed to a different map. "*Mexico*. That fool Maximilian, declaring himself the Austro-Hungarian Emperor of America and demanding that we return Texas." He turned back to West and Gordon. "And of course, the Navajo, the Cheyenne, the Apaches, the Nez Percé, and up in Dakota Territory, Sitting Bull and all those thousands of unhappy Sioux.

"And on top of all that"—Grant dipped a hand into his jacket pocket and withdrew another piece of paper—"we now have to deal with *this*." Grant held out the letter to West. Gordon snatched it, unfolded it, and read it aloud:

"*General Grant, the scientists that you seek are in my employ, and have created a weapons system beyond the pale of contemporary imagination. History and justice are on my side. I suggest you put your affairs in order, for in one week's time I will demand the unconditional surrender of the U.S. government.*"

Gordon stopped reading and turned the letter over. "It's not signed," he noted.

Grant directed Gordon's attention to a nearby glass case. "The letter was delivered inside this." The case contained a cake in the shape of the White House.

Gordon cocked an eyebrow at the cake. "Marzipan, isn't it?" He started to open the case and reach inside.

Grant grabbed his sleeve. "*Wait!*" An instant later a swarm of large and deadly-looking black spiders boiled out the windows and doors of the pastry White House, and an alarmed Gordon jerked his hand back and hastily shut the case.

West stepped forward. "It's McGrath, sir. He means to make the South rise again, and I'm gonna stop it."

Gordon shook his head. "Sir, West's obsession aside, McGrath may be a vicious killer, but a mastermind he is not. *This* . . ." He pointed at the spider-covered cake, and shuddered. Regaining his composure, he went on. "Reports from Intelligence indicate that the missing scientists may be incarcerated near Nashville. Given this lunatic's threat, I recommend a plan—"

West interrupted. "Forget that. Here's a better plan: nail McGrath's fat butt. Take him out and the whole thing collapses. We know this mastermind needs McGrath for whatever plot he's hatching, we know he's gonna make his move in one week, and we know McGrath is on his way to New Orleans. The longer we stand here talkin', the more of a head start he gets. I don't need no 'Intelligence' to tell me that."

Gordon couldn't resist. "Ah, so that would mean that you rely on 'Stupidity'?"

Grant, finally, had had enough. "*We do not have time for this childish bickering!*

"I am leaving for Utah in the morning. The Union Pacific and Central Pacific railroad-construction crews are about to meet at Promontory Point." Grant pointed across the room, to a large map of the United States. Two railroad lines had been drawn in, one in blue and one in red, with a small gap between them.

"For the first time, the United States will be truly *united*. That transcontinental railroad is going to be the . . . *commercial superhighway* that binds this great nation together! Think of it as a bridge to the twentieth century. It will bring together people of vastly different backgrounds, different cultures, different colors. People like . . . *you two.*"

Grant turned and fixed both West and Gordon with the same stare. "You two are the best I've got. You must put aside your personal differences and solve this *together.* If you don't, and if you fail . . . well, then we may never find out how great America could have been."

There was a reason why Grant had won both the Civil War and the 1868 election: He was a born leader. West and Gordon both stood silent a moment, sobered by the idea that Grant had just laid out and the responsibility he had just laid upon them.

Grant stepped forward and shook Gordon's hand. "I've put a private train at your disposal. Engine Number Five, Track Six." He turned and shook West's hand. "Go make sure that the South does *not* rise again." He snapped off a crisp West Point salute. "Dis-*missed!*"

As West reflexively returned Grant's salute and marched away, a prim female aide walked up with a small wrapped box and handed it to Gordon. "Here's the item you requested," she said. Gordon took the box and hurried after West.

CHAPTER FOUR

West untied the horse from the hitching post, slipped his silver-handled cane into the saddle rifle scabbard, stuck his left foot into the stirrup—

And stopped, to stare. Gordon was rolling out some kind of complicated jumped-up *velocipede*.

West shook his head in disgust. "Figures."

Gordon caught West looking at him and smiled proudly. "Impressive, isn't it? I call it the Bi-Axle Nitro Combust—"

"Save it," West snapped. "I'm in a hurry." He swung up into the saddle and backed the horse out. Then he looked down at Gordon, who was busy attaching the box he'd received in the War Room to a basket behind the seat of his bi-nitro whatchamacallit, and a wicked smile spread across West's face.

"But tell you what," West said. "You just pack your

little picnic lunch there, put up your parasol, and take your sweet time. I got a train to catch." He favored Gordon with one last smug smile, then put the spurs to the mustang and blasted off in a cloud of dust, a clatter of hooves, and a hearty, *"Yee-haaa!"* Moments later he was lost to sight, galloping madly through the traffic down Pennsylvania Avenue.

Gordon merely sighed, climbed onto the saddle of his velocipede, and took out a large handkerchief and began cleaning a pair of goggles. When he was satisfied with the goggles he slipped them over his face, opened the fuel line petcock, engaged the magneto, and rested his foot on the starter pedal.

"AVANT!"

Gordon kicked down hard on the starter pedal. The engine exploded to life with a throaty roar and a blast of fiery exhaust, and Gordon was instantly off with a neck-snapping jolt. Within moments he'd raced the engine up to its top speed and was grinding the transfer case over to its next set of gear ratios.

When he passed West slightly over a quarter mile later, Gordon barely even noticed it. He was thinking, *I really must find a smoother way to shift these gears. Perhaps some sort of spring-loaded plate, faced with an asbestos compound, could be used to temporarily disconnect the power train while the engine remains running . . .*

West rode hell-for-leather down a dirt road that ran beside the railroad track. He had to admit that from this angle, the private train looked like a beauty. The locomotive, *No. 5*, was a symphony in steam and black steel, and the two gleaming passenger cars that trailed behind it would have done proud to any insanely rich man. But instead of a rich man the rearmost car held only Artemus Gordon, sitting by a large window, working on—

Oh, my God. He's sewing.

"Stop this train!" West shouted, straining to be heard over the engine's chuffing pistons and his horse's pounding hooves. "*You hear me?*" If Gordon heard West, he pretended not to. Gordon casually took another stitch.

"Look, I'm sorry I tried to ditch you back at the White House!" *No you're not!* West's conscience chided him. "That was wrong!" Gordon paused to admire his own handiwork, then resumed sewing. "Grant said we were 'sposed to work this case *together*, remember?" Gordon snipped the thread, tied off the end, and started on a new button.

West tried to give the horse another kick, then abruptly realized he'd hit the wall. The locomotive was accelerating. The horse had given West everything he had and it wasn't enough. Another few seconds of racing like this and the train would be out of reach, the horse would most likely pull up lame, and James West would be stuck out in the Virginia countryside with a ruined rental horse and lot of explaining to do to President Grant.

He's a good horse. Doesn't deserve to be beat like this. He'll find his way home. Making his decision in a split second, West kissed his damage deposit good-bye, lunged for a handrail on the aft car, and bailed out of the saddle. For a few moments he dangled precariously, before his feet managed to find purchase on a small metal stepping plate.

The plate, to West's great surprise, turned out to be a booby trap. As was becoming a habit lately, West found himself to be flying . . .

This time, though, West dropped through a sliding panel in the roof of the railroad car and landed in a nicely upholstered comfy chair. West registered the car's interior in a heartbeat: oak bar, crystal decanters, pool table, bookshelves, steam engine chuffing in the background, wheels and trucks below the floor rumbling along the steel railroad track—

Gordon!

Artemus looked up from the leather-fringed jacket he was sewing. "Thanks for dropping in," he said calmly.

West bounced to his feet, veins bulging out in his forehead, fists clamping and unclamping like a pair of spasmodic hearts. "*That* does *it!*" West stripped off his jacket and threw it on the cabin floor. "*No more beards, bikes, or fake boobies!*" West popped off his cuff links and rolled up his sleeves. "*You put down that needle-point and let's settle this like* men!"

Gordon shrugged. "As a matter of clarification, this is not needlepoint." He nodded at a sampler on the wall. "That is." Gordon lifted his handiwork as if to show it to West. "Right now I'm putting the final touches on a new invention of mine. I call it the *Impermeable Waist-coat*. It's a vest that, when worn under the clothing, can stop any modern bullet, even when fired at close range."

West whipped out a gun and pointed it at Gordon's belly. "Really?"

Gordon hastily put the vest aside. "But it hasn't been tested empirically yet."

West reholstered his pistol, unbuckled his gun belt, and dropped it on a convenient chair. "*Get up!*" he ordered.

Gordon yawned. "Guns. I find them so primitive. And completely unnecessary, if one has done one's proper planning."

West dropped into a boxer's crouch and put up his dukes. "Yeah? And how do you feel about *fists*?"

Gordon sighed and got to his feet. "I must tell you, Captain West, I've always felt that allowing a situation to degenerate into physical violence indicates a failure on my part."

"Well then, Mr. Gordon, you *failed*!" West punctuated the sentence with a fast left jab at Gordon. Gordon flinched and backed away. West feinted another swing, then rolled the motion into a pivot kick. Gordon dodged it easily, but smiled slightly.

"Ah," Gordon said. "I see you're a student of the oriental arts. Personally, I prefer the more pacifistic form of *aikido*." West fired another kick at Gordon. Gordon turned, dodged, and gave West a small nudge just *so*, which sent him stumbling off the other way. "Wherein the Taoist principle of nonresistance is used to cause an opponent's own momentum to work against him," Gordon continued seamlessly.

West recovered his footing and spun around. There was murder in his eyes and steam coming out of his ears. *"What does it say about fixing a broken neck?"* West charged like an insane bull with fists. Gordon neatly dodged all the punches except the last one, which bloodied his lip.

Gordon dabbed at the blood in surprise, then shook his head. "I'm sorry, West, but you've brought this on yourself." To West's utter amazement, Gordon put his hands together as if praying, stood on one leg, storklike, then gracefully bent at the waist and darted a gentle kick at the wall.

Gordon's toe hit another concealed switch. A spring-loaded rawhide mallet popped out from wall and caught West hard in the side of the head, sending him spinning onto the pool table.

"Have you had enough?" Gordon asked innocently. "Shall we call it a draw?"

To Gordon's surprise, West shook the blow off and started coiling up to launch another attack. Realizing he was running out of tricks, Gordon decided to end it quickly. He thumbed a hidden button on the pool cue rack.

The pool table instantly revolved into the floor. In its place, there stood a rack loaded with weapons. Gordon shook his head in admiration. "I love this train!"

*   *   *

Meanwhile, on the underside of the car, Jim West was clinging to the truss rods, watching the railbed race by inches from his head and beginning to reconsider his approach. Maybe there was some validity to this idea of *planning*. He looked up and began to study the amazing complication of wires, hoses, and pneumatic actuators that underlay the cabin floor.

Gordon uncorked a fine Bordeaux, poured himself a glass, and stepped over to the weapons rack. *"The president, you know,"* he shouted at the floor, *"asked for my suggestions . . ."* Gordon tried a sip of wine. "Ah," he said to himself, "a mildly dry vintage of no particular breeding, but with an amusing presumption." He strolled over to the easy chair and settled in. *". . . on how to make the* Wanderer *both comfortable and functional—"*

Suddenly steel shackles popped out of the arms of the chair, pinning Gordon's wrists. An instant later the chair flipped over and Gordon found himself face-to-face with West, who was holding a handful of pneumatic tubes. The wineglass, in strict compliance with the law of gravity, emptied itself.

"Well, it's damn functional," West said calmly. "Anybody can see that."

Gordon struggled to fake the appearance of being calm. "Indeed. Has it perhaps occurred to you also that our methods do share a certain congruity, and that the president was right to pair us together? There may indeed by a synergy to be gained—"

The chair and the pool table flipped over simultaneously.

Back on the good side of the floor again, West and Gordon suddenly found themselves confronted by a scowling, grizzled old man in a rumpled and soot-stained blue suit—obviously, the train's engineer. There was fire in his eye, a stub of a hand-rolled cigarette in the corner of his mouth, and a large and steaming copper kettle in his leather-gloved hands.

"*Knock each other about all ya please, but harm another wire or tube on my train, and I'll douse ya like dogs!*"

Gordon's jaw dropped. "Hey! That's my veal reduction sauce!"

The engineer handed the steaming kettle to Gordon, who gratefully took it—then immediately set it down and began blowing on his scorched fingertips. The engineer looked at Gordon, shook his head, then took his gloves off and offered a handshake to West.

"Name's Coleman, Captain West," he said, between puffs on the cigarette. "And never mind what Gordon says: The *Wanderer* is my baby. Now"—he paused, for another drag on the cigarette—"let's get down to business, shall we? Where to?"

"*Nashville!*" said Gordon.

"*New Orleans!*" said West. They glared at each other

a moment. Coleman put his gloves back on and started reaching for the steaming kettle.

"Wait," Gordon said, in a reasonable and conciliatory tone. "Let's let Professor Morton decide."

West wrinkled his nose. "*Who?*"

Coleman went back to his work. Gordon led West through the parlor car and into the forward car, which was outfitted as a workshop. West recognized Gordon's nitro-velocipede; he recognized the chemists' and electromagneticist's equipment; he even recognized the laboratory workbench and the now-open box that Gordon had received in the White House War Room.

What threw him was the bearded human head clamped in a vise.

Gordon bowed as if making an introduction. "Captain West? May I present the late Professor Thaddeus Morton, formerly of M.I.T. An expert in the field of metallurgy, Professor Morton disappeared six months ago, and turned up in a field outside of Nashville two days ago. Or rather his head and body turned up, separated by a distance of about ten yards."

West, who had seen plenty of horrors on the battlefield, still gulped. "*That's* what was in that box?"

Gordon shrugged, and lifted up a strange metal ring. "That, and this. A magnetic collar, which was around the poor soul's neck just above the point of amputation. Haven't quite figured this one out yet." Gordon set the ring down.

West, meanwhile, was still staring bug-eyed at the

head. "Artemus, that is a man's *head*. You can't just take it apart like a broken cuckoo clock!"

Gordon dimmed the overhead lights and began fiddling with a projection lantern positioned behind Morton's head.

"Have you ever heard of the Retinal Terminus Theory?" Gordon asked. "It posits that a dying person's last conscious image is burned into the back of the eyeball, like a photograph." Satisfied with one aspect of the lantern, Gordon focused the light into two holes drilled in the back of Morton's skull. Two parallel beams of light emerged from Morton's eyes, to form a blurry color image on the opposite wall of the car.

"Morton's last image!" Gordon cried in delight.

"You're going to Hell for this," West said. "You know that, don't you?" Abruptly, West realized that the image was upside down, and cocked his head sideways to try to make sense of it.

Gordon recognized the problem. "Ah. The refraction of Morton's lenses causes the image to appear upside down. We simply . . ." He flipped the head in the vise. It was right-side-up now, but still badly out of focus. Gordon plucked the head out of the vise and began moving it back and forth, attempting to find the focal point.

He found it. An image leapt out at them: a hand, holding a bloody metal boomerang. In the background there was the shoulder and breast of a dark blazer or jacket, and a bearded head with a tiny brass horn in place of a left ear.

"*Voilà!*" said Gordon. "Morton's murderer!"

"It's McGrath," West said. "I was right all along."

"There seems to be a note in McGrath's coat pocket," Gordon noted. "It's still too fuzzy to read, though."

Light spilled into the lab; someone had slid open the door. Coleman walked in carrying a silver dinner tray. "Anybody hungry in here?" he asked.

West pointed at Morton's head. "Not me. Try him." Coleman looked where West was pointing.

He set the tray down and began backing for the door. "Eat hearty, gentlemen."

Gordon ignored Coleman; he was drumming his fingers on Morton's forehead and muttering to himself. "Hmm. Mortification of the *aqueous humor* seems to have led to a degradation—"

West's split-second decision-making process kicked in again. He looked at the head, looked at the projected image on the wall, remembered the photographs on the bulletin board in the War Room, and looked at Coleman.

"Glasses," West said. He snatched the spectacles from Coleman's breast pocket and handed them to Gordon. "Professor Morton wore glasses." Gordon held the glasses in front of Morton's eyes. The image sprang into clear focus.

"There." West pointed to a small bit of white protruding from the jacket pocket. Gordon pulled the head back to increase the projection size and fine-tuned the focus. West stepped in closer, and read, " 'Friends of the South! The pleasure of your company is requested at a Surprise Costume Ball at 8:30 P.M. on April 14, at 346 Garden Street, by the Wild Tchoupitoulas. . . . ' "

Gordon blinked. "The Wild Tchoupitoulas? Why does that name resonate? Perhaps, Borneo . . . ?"

West looked at him. "*Borneo?* Gordon, tchoupitoulas are wildflowers that grow all over southern Louisiana." He turned to Coleman.

"Like I said. New Orleans."

CHAPTER FIVE

The Louisiana bayou country is bald cypress swamp, mostly, pockmarked by the occasional stagnant catfish pond, alligator wallow, and yellow-fever mosquito-breeding pit. When the British army conquered the French Acadians in Nova Scotia in 1713 they immediately set about looking for the most miserable possible place they could conveniently dump the troublesome 'Cadians, and in 1755, they found it: a small French colony deep in the bayou backwaters, named for the ducal regent of France: *Nouvelle Orléans*.

In 1762 the French government secretly pawned the entire area off on Spain. In 1800 the Spanish succeeded in giving it back to France again. In 1802 President Thomas Jefferson sent statesman James Monroe to Paris to negotiate Mississippi River access rights, and was somewhere between surprised and stunned when the

French offered to sell him the whole kit and kaboodle for fifteen million dollars, cash. Jefferson, not realizing the offer also included the descendants of the Acadians—or as they called themselves now, Cajuns—jumped at the offer.

The French laughed all the way to the bank.

The night was hot and muggy, as it so often is in New Orleans when it isn't pouring rain. James West finished his recon sweep of the French Quarter and worked his way back to the railyard. The *Wanderer* sat parked on a little-used siding, gleaming in the pale moonlight: Coleman nodded briefly in acknowledgment of West's arrival, then disappeared around the farside of the No. 5 locomotive, no doubt oiling or polishing something. West climbed the steps of the rear car, taking care to avoid the booby traps and hidden switches that Gordon had been kind enough to point out to him earlier.

He found Gordon in the stateroom, standing before an enormous open wardrobe cabinet, wearing a dressing gown and rummaging through a vast array of costumes and disguises.

West put his cowboy hat back on his head and eyed the door. "I am not gonna wait around until you decide what frock to wear."

Gordon stopped shuffling through the costumes. "I wasn't looking for me." He spotted something that made him smile, then grabbed a hanger and pulled out a full livery costume. "How about this? You could go as my colored manservant."

West gritted his teeth, but made a conscious effort not to punch Gordon's lights out.

Gordon ignored West's reaction and admired the costume. "You won't need any guns. These buttons are actually hollow glass pellets, containing a powerful gas which temporarily freezes the human nervous system."

West scowled. "I am *not* going without a gun."

Gordon shrugged. "Very well. If you insist on carrying a firearm . . ." He broke into a grin and snatched a thick leather belt from the back of the wardrobe. The belt sported a massive, ornate, silver buckle. "Look!" Gordon tapped the buckle a certain way. The lid sprang open and deposited a derringer into Gordon's hand.

West blinked. "Uh, Gordon? Maybe you should lay off the Bordeaux for a while."

Gordon turned on West with an arched eyebrow and a tiny sneer. "Really? And what's your plan for crashing an invitation-only costume party full of drunken Southern sympathizers?"

"I plan to sneak in, kill McGrath, then retire, buy a farm, and raise peaches."

Gordon shook his head emphatically. "No, wrong! *We* go in, and, working together, we surreptitiously gather intelligence so that we can find and rescue the kidnapped scientists. To do this, Jim, we need *disguises*."

West took a step closer, looked through the wardrobe, and selected a black harlequin's mask, which he tied across his face.

"Okay, how 'bout this?"

Gordon sputtered. "Oh, great. Now you're a *masked*

black man wearing a pair of Army Colts and crashing an invitation-only costume party full of drunken Southern sympathizers. I like it. It's got shock value."

West shook his head. "Gordon, how can I let you down easy? You are not the expert on disguises you seem to think you are. Like, that night at Fat-Can's: I knew you weren't a woman. You may have a college education and all, but you don't know *nothing* about a woman's body."

The implicit challenge got Gordon's attention. "Really. Please instruct."

"You ever watch a woman walk?" West's voice and movements turned soft and sultry, as if he was describing someone special from memory. "When she takes a step, her body goes up, but her breasts go down. They jiggle like that 'cause they're soft and supple, and kinda flow. They're not two pieces of cast iron, sticking out like the Dahlgren cannons on the *Monitor*." West opened his eyes, caught himself, and reverted to normal form.

Gordon seemed thoughtful. "I used bean bags, but maybe a liquid would work better." Gordon shook his right hand, and a pen popped out of his right sleeve and into his hand. Then he shook his left hand, and a small notepad popped out of his left sleeve. West leaned closer, trying to catch a better glimpse of the spring-loaded gizmos up Gordon's sleeves.

"Cute. Why not carry a gun and a knife instead?"

Gordon frowned. "It has no poetry." Gordon tapped the pen point on the paper a few times, to get the ink flowing. "But you did give me one good idea." He began writing on the pad, and muttering while he wrote. "Breast bags should be filled not with plain water, but with a suspension: perhaps saline solution? They could be called . . . Mammarian HydrOxySal . . . inators."

West interjected. " 'Falsies' is too simple, huh?" Gordon ignored him, and with another odd little flip of the wrist, retracted the pen and notepad.

"Say!" Gordon said brightly. "With your advanced understanding of the fairer sex, perhaps *you* should be the one to go as a woman tonight!" He grabbed a low-cut, tasseled, and sequined blue dress from the wardrobe and turned around to show it to West.

West leaned in close to Gordon's face, and dropped his voice to a low and venomous rasp. "Gordon?

"I'd. Rather. Be. Dead."

Three Forty-six Garden Street turned out to be a large and stately old mansion near Lake Pontchartrain, well away from the noise and lights of the Vieux Carré. A wall surmounted by a wrought-iron fence surrounded the grounds, and a sizable number of men in Confederate uniforms patrolled the fence, but a noisy party was in progress on the veranda and the front gates stood open to admit a series of horse-drawn carriages.

Okay, Jim. Nothing like a frontal assault. West carefully watched the carriages move through the gate, timed the patterns of the guards, waited for exactly the right moment . . .

Now! West scampered out, ducked under the rear apron of a large brougham, and rode it through the gates. When he judged the carriage had completed the turn at the top of the driveway and was temporarily out of sight of the crowd on the veranda, he quietly dropped to the ground and rolled into the shadows. Taking a moment to get his bearings, he stood up.

Oops. West found himself standing face-to-face with a large guard who was carrying an even larger gun. The guard chuckled. It was not a friendly chuckle.

"You got as much chance of having an invitation as him," the guard said, jerking a thumb at the cast-iron lawn jockey.

West merely nodded. "Why, yassuh. As a matter of fact, I do has an invitation." He reached inside his jacket. "I gots it right here." He pulled his hand out again. *Watch the birdie!* The guard blinked at West's empty hand, uncomprehending.

"Huh? Wha—"

West's left jab caught the guard square on the jaw and sent him flying into the lawn jockey, where the side of the guard's head met the lawn jockey's outstretched hand with a resounding *clang!* that, presumably, came from the lawn jockey.

Mildly surprised at how quickly the fight was over, West looked around to see if anyone else had noticed, then dragged the unconscious guard over and leaned him against the side of the house. Using the guard's shoulders and head as an improvised stepladder, he scaled the side of the house, grabbed the ornamental ironwork, and vaulted over the railing to a second-floor balcony.

French doors, good. The small pane of glass next to the lockwork shattered easily, and no one seemed to notice the sound over the fireworks and party noise. West reached through, unlocked the door, and slipped inside. There was a thick curtain between the door and the room.

West heard women's voices on the other side of the curtain, and froze.

"Get your hands off me!" one voice shrieked. "Put me down in the dungeon with all those smelly old men, but I am not going in *there!*" The voice was young, defiant, and marked by an upper-class Spanish accent.

"Do not be selfish and stupid," another woman said. Her voice was slightly older and had a Germanic edge. "You should be tickled to be his new favorite."

"Oh yeah? Well *that* doesn't look like it tickles!"

A third voice cut in, this time with a bit of a French accent. "It is not so bad once the metal warms up."

"I'm an entertainer, not a *puta!*" There was the sound of a sharp slap.

Curiosity got the better of West. He carefully edged over to a small gap in the curtains, and peered out. Three women—three *large* women, in tall wigs and elaborate Empire dresses—seemed to be engaged in dragging a dark-eyed Latina beauty toward a side door. Through the partially open door, West glimpsed an enormous four-poster bed, beneath and surrounded by an insanely complex assembly of belts, straps, pulleys, manacles, and steel rods.

The tallest blonde woman appeared to be holding the gasping Latina by the throat. "He *loves* us," the blonde growled.

"That's why . . . I don't want you . . . getting jealous,"

the Latina answered. West began to feel an irresistible
urge to do something.

Remember Fat Can Candy's, the inner voice of his
good sense advised. *You don't know what's really going
on here. 'Sides, that blonde looks like she could bench
press a beer wagon.* West decided to give the scene a few
more seconds to play out.

The Amazon released the Latina. The four of them
proceded in concert into the bedroom and shut the door.
West slipped out from behind the curtain, considered the
closed door a moment, then headed in the other direction,
shaking his head.

The ballroom was grand, ornate, and lavishly decorated.
The costumed crowd, an exclusive assemblage of
wealthy Southern aristocracy and arrogant European
minor nobility. The music?

Well, that was just plain annoying, but West figured
there was no accounting for taste. He slipped from the
shadows, ducked behind a pillar, and edged out onto the
balcony to survey the crowd below.

"Oh my," a sultry female voice behind him exclaimed,
"an authentic cowboy costume. Complete with guns!"

West turned around, slowly, as if he had every right to
be there. The woman who'd busted him was one seriously *fatale* femme; Chinese, utterly beautiful, and wearing a striking red silk Dragon Lady dress. She stepped
forward and reached out to touch his hat. "What a terribly clever costume, Mr. . . . ?"

"West," West said. "James West."

The Dragon Lady smiled demurely. "Well then, West meets East. Mae Lee East." She curtsied, and offered West her delicate hand. The red polish on her long fingernails glistened like fresh blood. West took her hand and kissed it.

She smiled again. "Are you here alone, Mr. West?"

West glanced over his shoulder, at the crowd in the ballroom below. "Actually, I'm—uh, trying to surprise an old friend, General McGrath. I can't seem to find him here, though. Have you seen him?"

A troubled look crossed Miss East's face, and she tapped a finger to her perfect lips. "General McGrath? I don't remember that name being on the guest list. And I should know; I'm Dr. Loveless's personal assistant."

Loveless.

West caught his reaction a fractional second later, and willed his jaw muscles to relax and his lips to re-form into an insipid smile. "Ah yes, Dr. Arliss Loveless. One of the great founding fathers of the Confederate States of America. Funny how some people actually thought he was dead."

Mae Lee's smile was like the sunrise in the east, and she rewarded West with it again. "He's had a long and difficult recovery, true. But tonight is his coming-out party." She slipped a hand around West's elbow. "Shall we?" West took one last glance from the balcony, then let Mae Lee lead him down the stairs and into the crowd.

It took West all of thirty seconds to spot Gordon. He'd gone for the "Dora" costume again: big hair, sleazy dress, prominent fake beauty spot on his cheek. *Predictable*, West's inner voice sighed.

The dance music stopped abruptly, then the musicians played a dramatic little fluorish. "Uh-oh," Mae Lee said, "pumpkin time." She blew West a kiss. "Meet me later, in the foyer." She scampered off. West's eyes tracked her across the ballroom, until she joined up with—

Oh, Lordy. Those three female wrestlers from upstairs.

The women took their places in front of a large doorway. Mae Lee blew a note on a pitch pipe. The band struck up an introduction, and the four women began singing. *"Mine eyes have seen the glory of the coming of the Lord. . . ."* The singing almost, but not quite, covered a high-pitched whirring noise from behind the closed doors, followed by a mechanical *clunk.* Suddenly, the doors swung open, and a miniature parade float rolled into the room, apparently under its own power. In papier mâché and flowers, the float depicted President Abraham Lincoln, sitting in a theater box.

Now that *is tacky*, West thought. But he noticed that everyone else around him was laughing and pointing, so he forced out a grin and a chuckle.

The singing women stepped out in front of the float and marched before it, strewing red grapes on the floor. *"He has trampled down the vineyard where the grapes of wrath are stored."* The float rolled over the grapes, crushing them and making a merry mess of the ballroom floor. West cocked his head to try to get a better look at the float's undercarriage. His nostrils flared at the faint scent of a familiar, sulphury, odor.

KA-BOOM!

Lincoln's head exploded like a piñata, showering the party goers with hard candies and bits of shredded paper. A ghastly hush instantly fell across the room.

Pause.

An impishly grinning face popped up through the smoking hole where Lincoln's head had been. "Don't you just *hate* that song?" he asked, exulting. The audience gasped in recognition.

"Why, y'all look like you've just seen a *ghost*," the man in the float continued cheerfully. "It's *me*, friends, alive and kicking! Well, alive, anyway . . ."

The audience erupted in applause and laughter. James West forced himself to join in, briefly. But inside he was thinking, *Dr. Arliss Loveless. Just let me catch you in a dark alley sometime, you little* . . . The audience fell silent. Loveless was speaking again.

"We may have lost the war," he said. "But heaven knows, we haven't lost our sense of humor!" This elicited another brief round of applause, while Mae Lee and the other women surrounded Loveless and began taking apart the Lincoln float.

The room fell silent again, this time with a sickened gasp or two. West blinked, and tried hard not to stare. Dr. Loveless was sitting in a wheelchair . . .

Or rather, *half* of him was. It was hard to tell for sure, what with all the mechanical bits and all, but it appeared that everything below the man's navel was just plain gone.

Loveless looked down at himself, smoothed the front

of his suit, and pursed his lips. "No, indeed we haven't." When he looked up again, his cheeks were flushed, and every last trace of smile was gone from his face. "Not even when we've lost a lung! A spleen! A bladder! Two legs, thirty-five feet of small intestine, and the ability to reproduce! *All in the name of the South!*" Loveless let his voice drop to a soft whisper. "Not even then, do we lose our sense of humor." The crowd fell into another, almost prayerful, hush. Loveless held them all spellbound a moment longer.

Then he cracked a toothy grin. "So! *Mi casa es su casa! Ma maison est à tu! Let the party begin!*" This, apparently, was the signal to the orchestra. The music resumed, the crowd broke up into laughter and conversation, and the drinks flowed like the Mississippi, only less muddy.

Mae Lee leaned over and whispered something in Loveless's ear. He turned his head and looked straight at West.

Uh-oh. The jig is up. Jim West straightened up, primed his wits, and prepared his best cocky smile. With Mae Lee's help, Dr. Loveless came rolling over.

"Well, well," Dr. Loveless said when he'd gotten within speaking range. "Lieutenant West. How nice of you to join us and add a little *color* to this evening."

West smiled. "It's Captain West, now. And when a man comes back from the dead, it's an occasion to *stand* and be counted."

Loveless shook his head slightly and *tch*-ed, as if to himself. "Captain? My word, Grant must be scraping the bottom of the barrel." He brightened up into a faux smile. "Miss East informs me that you were expecting to find General McGrath here. Sorry, but I haven't seen him in a *coon's* age."

West's molars ground, but he kept his smile. "I'm not surprised. I bet a man like you finds it difficult to keep in touch with even *half* the people you know."

Loveless's eyes flashed angrily. "Perhaps the lovely Miss East will keep you from being a *slave* to your disappointment."

West shrugged. "Well, you know beautiful women. They encourage you one second, then cut the legs out from under you the next."

Loveless's smile faltered, then collapsed. He abruptly wheeled his chair about and steamed away. Mae Lee offered Jim a helpless little smile, then scampered after Loveless.

West waited a cautious interval, then set off in an oblique, looping path through the ballroom, carefully tailing Loveless. By pure coincidence he happened to be standing near "Dora" when he caught a glimpse of Loveless conversing with McGrath in a side corridor. The two men went into a study and closed the doors.

West turned to Dora. "Hey, your little doggie is here. But this time, *I'm* the one who'll get him to speak." He gave Dora a mocking growl and headed off into the corridor.

*   *   *

After West left, Miss Tammy Jo Farraday, of 834 Helena Lane, Baton Rouge, turned to her date, and said, "Who the hell was *that*?"

Twenty yards away, Artemus Gordon, who was dressed as a mountain man in a fringed buckskin jacket, shook his head, put down his drink, and decided he'd better follow West.

CHAPTER SIX

The desk in the study was a highly polished mahogany affair, large enough to double as a banquet table for twelve. Loveless sat on one side of it, toying with a pencil. McGrath paced the other side, like an obese panther in a small cage.

"Dr. Loveless, my men are ready to go to war, but we can't fight without weapons! Ever since those munitions were destroyed in West Virginia, lice and demoralization have set in!"

Loveless looked up from his desk and smiled. "Never despair, General. Your men will receive new weapons tonight. I've a ship standing offshore with the finest guns my Continental associates can supply, and I promise you, *tonight*, your men will become part of the greatest military victory of this century!"

McGrath stopped pacing, relaxed with a sigh, and broke into a grin. "Oh, you're a pip, sir! I'd follow you into the maw of Cerberus himself!"

"And so you shall, General." Loveless slid a sheet of paper nearer and began drawing a map. "Have your men meet us *here*"—he drew an X—"at precisely ten o'clock." McGrath took the paper, nodded, and stuffed it into his pocket. Loveless backed his wheelchair away from the desk and headed for the door.

West waited in the shadows until Loveless and McGrath were back amongst the crowd in the ballroom, then slipped over to the study door, drew a thin metal lockpick from his hatband, and popped the lock. A moment later he was inside and silently shutting the door behind himself.

West took a few seconds to case the room. Besides the desk, it featured some bookshelves, assorted *objets de junque*, and way too many overblown oil portraits of various Loveless ancestors and relatives. *Inbred bunch*, West thought. Especially that guy in the huge full-length painting that hung behind the desk, standing there with his dogs and his shotgun and a bunch of dead grouse and all. West got the strangest feeling that the painting was somehow looking at him.

He shook it off and turned his attention to the desk. There was a faint imprint on the blotter where Loveless had drawn the map. West picked up the pencil and a penknife, grated some graphite onto the blotter, found another sheet of paper, and was just about to do a rubbing when someone snatched the paper out of his hand. West spun, hand already on the butt of his Colt.

Mae Lee East was standing there, waving a finger at West in the classic "naughty, naughty" gesture.

"I said to meet me in the *foyer*," she said.

West smiled. "Oh, the *foy-aay*. Sorry, I've never been much good at French."

East grabbed him by the hair and slapped a passionate kiss on his mouth. Her tongue made it clear back to his wisdom teeth.

After a while, she let him come up for air. "*Au contraire*," she said. "You're very good at it." Leading him by the lower lip, she pushed him into a convenient chair. "So let's see, Mister West. Are you a dangerous spy of some sort? Or just a handsome cowboy who likes to . . . poke around?" She began unbuttoning the fly of his trousers.

"Um." West slipped a gear. "Uh, that second one. Yeah."

Gordon watched West slide into the study, then decided the best way to cover West's butt was to return to the party and keep an eye on Loveless. He moved through the crowd discreetly, chatting here, nodding and smiling there, playing the perfect amiable guest.

An elderly man in a powdered wig and a younger woman costumed as Marie Antoinette caught his eye. Gordon sidled up to them. "*Bonsoir, monsieur et madame . . . eh, Antoinette?*" The woman smiled, but the older man regarded him with an icy glare.

"What can I do for you?" the man responded.

Gordon continued in French. "Well, I was just wondering what the distinguished Army Minister of France could find so compelling in New Orleans when his own country is teetering on the brink of war with Prussia?"

The Army Minister blanched and led his partner away.

Gordon turned and began scanning the crowd for a new victim. A bit of movement on the balcony caught his eye: Loveless's three amazon warriors, coming out of an upstairs bedroom and locking the door behind themselves. He immediately equated "locked door" with "interesting," and started for the stairs.

The tall blonde dockworker-type woman blocked his way. "Well howdy there!" Gordon said, switching accents like a verbal chameleon. "I like a big, sturdy gal! Is yer dance card full?"

The Amazon snarled something at him in Extremely Low German. Gordon shrugged and went back to the party.

West found the situation . . . *challenging.* On the one hand, he and Mae Lee were lip-locked in a passionate embrace, and make no mistake about it: She was very good at passionate. But on the other hand, he *really* wanted to get that rubbing of Loveless's map before anything else left an impression or wet spot on the desk blotter.

Here's an idea, his inner voice suggested. And for once, his impulsive side agreed. He slipped a hand up under her skirt.

She gasped, and kissed him harder.

He got his other hand up there, and hiked her hemline up around her waist.

She moaned, and gnawed on his earlobe.

He maneuvered her over to the desk, and parked her perfect little fanny on the blotter.

She trembled in anticipation, and spread her thighs.

Very carefully, West stood up, and pulled her to her feet.

Confused, Mae Lee tried to figure out what West was up to and how to follow suit.

Craning his neck, he looked over her shoulder. She assumed this was a request for more kissing and went for his jugular.

Ah, got it! I got the map imprint on her butt! Except, wait . . . aw Hell, it's backwards! West spotted a full-length mirror across the room and started maneuvering her toward it. Finally, he got a good look at the map, and all became clear: the weapons were going to be delivered at Malheureux Point, northeast of New Orleans.

West sighed with satisfaction. Plenty of time to finish the business with Miss East and still make it to the rendezvous. His intelligent inner voice thanked his impulsive side for its cooperation and turned it loose to have some fun.

A flicker of movement in the mirror caught West's eye. That big ugly painting behind the desk: The gun barrels were moving! In a split second of action West threw himself to the side and drew his Colt —

The gun behind the painting went off an instant before

West's pistol, but the assassin missed, and West's shot
went true, and the gunman fell through the torn canvas,
very dead. Relieved to find himself unhurt, West turned
back to Mae Lee, a cocky quip on his lips.

Whatever he was going to say, it died there, along with
Mae Lee East, who lay sprawled across the desk with a
single round and bloody bullet hole through her forehead.
Gently, Jim West eased her body to the floor and covered
her decently. Then he ejected the spent cartridge from his
pistol, loaded a fresh one, buttoned up his fly, and headed
back to the party, all the while hoping that no one had noticed the gunshots over the sounds of the fireworks outside.

Miss Tammy Jo Farraday, of 834 Helena Lane, Baton
Rouge, was terrified. One moment she was dancing with
her date, and the next moment this strange and angry
black man had cut in and was more dragging than dancing with her.

"I'm real impressed with the way you got the dance
floor staked out," he growled, marching her across the
floor. "Maybe one of your missing scientists will cut in."
The music was a Kentucky reel. They dipped and turned.

"But I thought you should know, while you were trying to decide what shoes to wear, I learned a couple interesting little things." Dip, and twirl.

"Our host, Dr. Loveless," West nodded over to the
side, to where Loveless was leading a contingent of foreign nationals out the side door, "has a shipment of guns

and ammo coming in tonight and is meeting McGrath at Malheureux Point in an hour." Pause, and bend.

"So enjoy the party, Cinderella. Me, I gotta go save the Republic."

Miss Tammy Jo Farraday, of 834 Helena Lane, Baton Rouge, was utterly speechless.

"But I must say," West added, "you've really improved those beanbags. They look damn perky." He grabbed them both and gave them a little squeeze.

Miss Tammy Jo Farraday froze in shock, let out a shriek that shattered three champagne glasses, and gave Jim West a slap so hard it nearly made his head spin around like a turnstile. The music stopped. All motion stopped. For five deathly quiet seconds, James West was the absolute focus of every shocked white face in that room.

A mountain man in a fringed buckskin jacket stepped forward. "HANG HIM!" the man screamed. He pulled a rope from inside his jacket and threw it to the crowd.

It was at that moment that West finally recognized both Artemus Gordon and his own fatal mistake.

The angry lynch mob surged out the door, carrying Jim West. Artemus Gordon calmly straightened his coonskin cap, adjusted his buckskin jacket, and headed for the back stairs. The upstairs bedroom door wasn't guarded. His Auto-Mecha-Pick-o-Matic made short work of the lock.

West was definitely having a bad evening. They'd grabbed his guns and knife immediately, of course, and promptly found a sturdy lamppost for the lynching. But it was all the rampaging yokels with torches and pitchforks who really made it a corker.

Someone threw Gordon's rope over the lamppost. Six other someones rolled a wagon up under the lamppost and stood West in the back of it. A man dressed as George Washington tied West's hands together behind his back.

"Looks like we're gonna have to learn ya'll a little lesson on how to behave in polite society," George said. He looped the noose over West's neck.

West tried a sickly grin. "Don't grab a white lady's boobs at the big redneck cotillion? Is that the lesson? Well, trust me, I learned it. Don't scratch your head with the shrimp fork? Hey, I got that one down, too. So whaddaya say we call this whole thing off?" He looked around the faces in the nearby mob, leering, evil, and ugly in the torchlight. He didn't seem to be getting any takers. . . .

Gordon eased into the darkened room. The star attraction seemed to be an enormous four-poster bed, surrounded by a bewildering assortment of belts, pulleys, manacles, and metal pipes. Beside the bed stood the largest birdcage Gordon had even seen, and inside the cage stood a beautiful young Latina woman in a skimpy camisole.

"Mister," she greeted Gordon, "you lay one stinking finger on me, and I'll bite it off!"

Gordon quickly held up his hands. "Madam, please! Stay calm! While I realize that I look like something straight out of James Fenimore Cooper—"

She wrinkled her nose. "Who?"

"My name is Artemus Gordon. I'm a U.S. Marshal. I'm here to help, and you look like you're in trouble."

Whoever the woman was and however she'd gotten there, she had not lost her sense of sarcasm. "Oh, really? What makes you say that?" She grabbed the locked gate of the cage and rattled it for emphasis. "Can you get me out of here?"

Gordon nodded. "I think so." He opened his jacket and began pulling out an assortment of miniature tools.

The woman watched him in strained amusement for a bit, then decided he was worth talking to. "Not that I'm complaining," she said, "but what the Hell are *you* doing here?"

Gordon continued assembling his tools. "I'm looking for some kidnapped scientists. I don't suppose you've seen any around here, have you?" He unsnapped the sole of his boot, and connected it to a thin cable looped around the spur on his heel. The other end of the cable connected to a pinion gear on a chuck and handle, and the final piece was a carbide drill bit. Gordon began pumping the foot pedal. The drill bit chewed into the metal around the lock.

Rita shook her head in disbelief. "Sure, I seen them. Who do you think came up with *that* stuff?" She nodded at the bed. "Loveless has 'em working in the cellar, with these weird collars on. Get me out of here, and I'll show you the way down there."

Gordon's ears perked up. "If they were all in the cellar, we're too late. The cellar is cleaned out. It was the first place I checked, right after I sampled the gumbo. A bit heavy on the okra." The drill cut through the final piece of metal, and the lock fell to pieces. Gordon opened the cage door and helped the obviously distressed damsel out.

"*Muchas gracias*," she said. "By the way, my name is Rita. I'm an . . . entertainer."

Gordon nodded. "Of course you are."

Things were not going at all the way Jim West had planned. The horses were getting antsy; the crowd members were practically drooling on their shirts in anticipation. "George" had pretty much proven himself immune to threats, reason, or common sense.

"*Do you have any last words, boy?*" George shouted.

"Would it help if I said I thought she was a man?"

Miss Tammy Jo Farraday gasped and fainted.

"Guess not," West said.

"*Hang him!*" George bellowed. The driver cracked the whip. The wagon lurched forward, to leave Jim West dancing on air. He hit the end of his rope. . . .

The rope stretched like saltwater taffy, to gently deposit West on the ground.

George and his four closest buddies were still trying to comprehend what the hell had happened when there came a scream from the back of the crowd, followed by a lot of shouting and pounding hooves. "*YEE-HAAA!*" George spun around.

West figured it out a second before anyone around him did. Artemus Gordon, in a stolen carriage, was driving straight into the middle of the lynch mob. West kicked George in the back, snatched a pistol from George's belt, and used the man's head as a springboard to somersault into the air and land in the back of the carriage as it raced past. Gordon whipped around with a bowie knife and severed the rope just as it started to grow taut again, then split the ropes binding West's wrists.

West leaned into Gordon's ear. "*Hang him?* HANG *him?*"

Gordon grinned. "Did it ever occur to you that my carefully planned diversion enabled me to search the house for the missing scientists?" The carriage careened around a corner on two wheels.

Rita joined in the shouting. "Artemus, if you're gonna drive like this, let me wear your coat! I'm freezing!"

West seemingly noticed Rita for the first time, then recognized her as the woman the Amazons had dragged into the bedroom. "So you're a scientist, huh?"

"I'm an entertainer."

"Yeah, right. And I'm a Chinese cook."

Satisfied that they were safely away from the crowd, Gordon slowed the horses to a fast trot and turned to them both. "Rita, meet Jim West. Jim, Rita. Loveless had her locked in a cage in his bedroom. Chivalry dictated that I couldn't leave her there." Gordon took his fringed jacket off and draped it over Rita's shivering shoulders. The carriage rounded another corner.

A half dozen of McGrath's men, with rifles, formed a skirmish line across the street before them.

Gordon ripped a handful of buttons off the fringed jacket and threw them into the midst of the rebs. The buttons burst in a cloud of quickly dissipating gas, instantly freezing the men into living statues.

"The pigeons always like that one," Gordon said smugly, as he drove the trotting horses through the line of petrified men.

West pushed Rita's head down. "Yeah, well, those pigeons better be able to hit moving targets. It's wearing off."

"*What?*" Gordon turned around to look. The first rifle shot spanged off the seat next to him.

"*Drive!*" West shouted. Gordon cracked the whip. West vaulted into the backseat and drew the pistol he'd taken from George. Rebel rifle bullets shredded the tonneau.

Jim West's pistol bullets shredded the rebs.

Another moment later and all was quiet, save for the creaking of the carriage springs and the clatter of galloping hooves on cobblestones. "I'm impressed," Rita said. "Maybe you can get Loveless to give me my money back, too. I paid for my own train ticket from Texas." Once again, Gordon slowed the horses to a canter.

West turned on Gordon. "Why do you keep *slowing down*? McGrath and Loveless are gonna meet at Malheureux Point in less than an hour!" Suddenly West vaulted over Rita, landed on the back of the left horse, and grabbed a handful of mane. Leaning over, West unclipped the harness, then gave the horse a kick in the ribs. "I ain't got time for you to play coachman for the lady! Catch up with me when you can!" he shouted at Gordon, as he galloped off into the night.

Rita climbed up on the seat next to Artemus. "Impetuous, isn't he?"

Gordon sighed. "You don't know the half of it."

CHAPTER SEVEN

The sidewheel steam yacht lay quietly at anchor, perhaps a quarter mile off the marshy shore of Malheureux Point. General McGrath stood at the starboard
rail, watching the moonlight glisten like oil on the calm
water, listening to the soft mutter of conversations on the
foredeck, and noting the occasional slap of a vagrant
wave against the wooden hull. The still night air was rich
with smells: woodsmoke from the yacht's idle boilers,
spices and grilled meats cooking in the galley, and the
strange, undefinable, but quite unforgettable scent of rotting vegetation, stagnant salt water, and swampy tidal
flats.

Disquiet gnawed at McGrath's gut like the fox in that
fable about the Spartan boy. Slowly and deliberately,
more in hopes of keeping himself distracted than out of

any actual desire, McGrath worked through his coat pockets, searching for his folding knife and a plug of chewing tobacco. Presently he found both and began to whittle off a chaw.

One of Loveless's stewards wandered by, carrying a silver tray laden with full champagne glasses. McGrath quickly pocketed the tobacco and knife and snagged two drinks instead. One he downed in a single gulp. The other he decided to save for later.

Introspection goes better with whiskey, McGrath thought, as he eased out a quiet belch. McGrath was not normally a man who had much truck with introspection, but the situation seemed to call for it now. *Loveless is up to something.*

But what?

The nagging sense of disquiet and dyspepsia returned.

True, Loveless had delivered on his promise. It was hard to do on such short notice, but McGrath had managed to round up most of the Louisiana Brigade and march them—the ones who were sober enough to walk, anyway—out to Malheureux Point. There, exactly as Loveless had described, they'd found a large round open meadow, surrounded by several stacks of long wooden crates. Breaking open the crates, they'd found the mother lode: row upon row of the finest rifles in all the world, and ammunition enough to start a major war.

But, British .450 Martini-Henrys? Spanish .43 Peabodys? French Chassepots, Prussian Dreyses, Danish Peterssons, and American Allin-Springfields in both .58 rimfire and .50-70? Any one of them alone was a superb rifle, but taken together, they presented McGrath with a logistical *nightmare.* He was still trying to figure out some sensible way to distribute the weapons when the Indian, Hudson, pulled him aside and told him Loveless had requested his presence on the yacht. Turning the job of doling out rifles over to Colonel Parker, McGrath followed Hudson down to the waterfront, where a rowboat and crew waited.

As McGrath now waited, cooling his heels while Dr. Loveless flattered and laughed with his foreign friends.

I owe Loveless everything, McGrath reminded himself. *If it weren't for him, I'd be robbing banks, like Frank James and his snot-nosed punk little brother.* That thought opened the door of memory and admitted the shades of old friends, now long since dead and gone. William Quantrill, who died in a Yankee prison. Henry Wirz, hanged for war crimes. John Mosby, who surrendered and reswore loyalty to the Union, which as far as McGrath was concerned made him even worse than dead. McGrath's only child, Euen, as fine a lad as ever lived, just sixteen years old when he was cut down by Yankee rifles in the "Hornet's Nest" at Shiloh.

His dear wife, Dorothea, murdered when Sherman's army marched through South Carolina and the great general decided to pause for a day, to let his soldiers rest, relax, and loot and burn the town of Columbia.

Another of Loveless's stewards walked by, this one carrying a platter of spicy grilled chicken wings. McGrath grabbed one, gnawed it down to greasy bones, then tossed the remains over the side and wiped his fingers on his coat.

I lost my wife. I lost my son. Unconsciously, Mc-Grath's fingers drifted up, to touch his prosthetic ear. *Damn near lost my* head *driving the Yankees out of Chickamauga, and three days later they came marching right back in.*

So why am I still fighting?

Certainly not for the South that was, and could never be again. Slavery was gone forever, not that McGrath cared. The McGrath family had never owned any slaves, and while McGrath had nothing personal against Negroes, he didn't have much use for them, either.

This thought strayed perilously close to another closed door in McGrath's memory. It was the last year of the war; the North was starting to field Negro regiments in increasing numbers. His Rebel boys usually made a decent effort at taking white captives alive and packing them off to Andersonville prison camp, where they stood at least a fair chance of surviving until the end of the war. But Negro prisoners seemed to bring out a special fury, and try as McGrath might he couldn't stop his men from using black prisoners for bayonet practice. But there were atrocities, and then there was *The Atrocity.* . . .

General McGrath abruptly remembered why he always avoided introspection. He downed the second glass of champagne, wished again for strong whiskey, and started looking for a place to set his empty glass down. He looked toward the foredeck.

Dr. Loveless detached himself from a conversation

with a pair of bristly-mustached Prussians and rolled his wheelchair over. "General!" he called out jovially, as if seeing him for the first time. "How good of you to join us!"

"Thank you for inviting me," McGrath said courteously. There were questions he needed to ask Loveless—important questions, such as how Loveless intended to accomplish with a thousand men what Robert E. Lee couldn't do with a quarter million—but this was not quite the place or time.

Another servant came by with more champagne. Loveless took a glass for himself and directed the man to give McGrath a refill. "Well, General," Loveless said, as he raised his glass in a toast. "It's been a long journey from New Liberty."

McGrath froze in mid-toast. "Sir, there is not a day that passes that I do not contemplate it."

With a little extra effort, Loveless closed the gap and clinked the glasses. "Yes, and so do I." Loveless sipped his champagne. "So do I," he repeated thoughtfully. He set the glass on the arm of his chair and attempted to rest a hand on the knee that wasn't there—caught himself, and shook his head wistfully. "If I'd only had then the scientific knowledge of explosives and primers that I have today . . ."

McGrath slowly turned and gave Loveless a baleful look. "That's not what I meant."

For a moment Loveless seemed puzzled, then he smiled. "Ah. You mean that stomach-turning carnage that earned you your unfortunate *nom de guerre*." He turned and raised his voice, so that all around might hear. "What was that nickname again?"

Aware that all eyes were on him, McGrath spoke, albeit in a reluctant mumble. "Bloodbath McGrath."

Loveless cupped a hand to his left ear, in cruel imitation of McGrath's prosthetic. "Come again, General?"

"*Bloodbath McGrath*," he repeated, this time with a certain loud defiance. "*The Butcher of New Liberty*."

Loveless smiled, as if somehow pleased by the angry reaction he'd elicited from McGrath, and turned his wheelchair to face the shore. "Munitia, dear?" The amazon with the French accent handed Loveless a pair of field glasses, then offered McGrath a second pair. McGrath declined.

Loveless glassed the shoreline and continued speaking. "You have assembled an impressive force, General. Seasoned combat veterans all." He lowered the field glasses for a moment and winked at Munitia, who slipped away. "My associates"—Loveless nodded in the general direction of the foreign crowd—"have supplied your men with the best military arms in the world."

The short, shrill blast of a steam whistle split the air—a signal, apparently. Munitia returned to Loveless's side.

"Now, General," Loveless said, grinning wickedly, "*behold the future!*"

As the yacht's whistle echoed across the bay, Colonel Parker snapped his pocket watch shut and slipped it back into his waistcoat. "What the blue blazes was *that* for?" he asked of no one in particular. He stepped away from the torchlight and the mob of men clustered around the rifles and tried to get a clearer look at the yacht. Another group of men hurried past him.

Parker spotted a single faded chevron on a threadbare gray jacket. "Corporal!"

Corporal Thug stopped and saluted. "Yessir?"

"Is General McGrath back from the boat yet?"

"Dunno, sir."

"Then detail some men to look for him. Get down to the waterfront and—" Parker froze. There seemed to be something moving down in the marsh, behind the corporal. Something *big*. "What the devil . . . ?"

A piercing, inhuman scream rent the air, and a mighty engine roared to life. Steam jets blasted; massive metal gears ground and clanked, and a great dark *something* the size of a small ship plowed headlong through the marsh, flattening all before it.

"Defensive positions!" Parker shouted. "You there! Set up a cross fire from behind them crates!" He pointed to another group of men. "You! Take the left flank!" He grabbed Corporal Thug. "Pass the word to lock and load, but hold off'n your fire 'til I gives the command!" The corporal dashed off. Parker drew his revolver and tried to find some cover, but aside from a stack of crates, there was none to be found.

"Can anybody see it?" Parker bellowed.

"Yassuh!" a voice off on the far right flank answered, shouting to be heard over the screeching and clanking. "It looks like . . . gol dang, sir, it's a *Monitor*! And it's just a-climbin' right up on dry land!"

Parker cocked his pistol. "Steady, boys!"

"Wait, sir!" the voice on the right flank shouted. "It's—it's a-wearin' the Stars and Bars! It's one of *ours*!" At this news the troops let fly a wild volley of cheers and Rebel yells. Parker uncocked his revolver, holstered it, and stepped out from behind the stack of crates.

"A land ironclad," he said softly. "Now ain't that a wonderment." Nervous, but excited, he began to walk toward it.

The thing was huge, fantastic, and in Parker's eyes, utterly beautiful. It looked like some great miscegenated offspring of a locomotive's drunken fling with a river gunboat, and it crawled on a pair of hoopsnakelike articulated caterpillar tracks. The hull wasn't mere iron or ordinary steel: It was some kind of wild new alloy that fairly glowed in the pale moonlight. The machine sported a rotating turret on top, housing what appeared to be about a six-inch ordnance rifle; a pair of cluster-barrel Gatlings, that waved like monstrous insect antennae; and a plethora of other, smaller, gun ports, fore and aft.

Colonel Parker couldn't wait to get into the driver's seat.

The clattering, roaring monster heaved up into the middle of the meadow and stopped. Steam vented with a giant teakettle screech, and the engines settled down into a massive low throb that Parker felt more through his feet than heard through his ears. A hatch popped open in the very top of the turret. Parker began to walk around to the stern, where he guessed the boarding ladder would be, but stopped when he clearly heard a female voice say, "*Los!*"

A signal rocket erupted from the top of the turret and burst overhead in a blinding white flash. For a few seconds every man in the meadow was thrown into sharp relief, as the parachute flare drifted lazily down. When Parker could see clearly again, he noticed that a Gatling had swiveled to point at him, and with an expert's eye he guessed it to be one of the new six-barrel .50-70 government models.

His last thought on Earth was, *I would purely love to hear that thing go off!*

McGrath stood at the starboard rail, staring in open-mouthed horror at the slaughter of his troops. The land ironclad's Gatlings mowed through the ranks like a scythe, while the ragged volleys of their return fire merely pinged off its gleaming hull like hail on a tin roof. One squad of soldiers seemed immune to the general terror and tried to make an improvised breastwork of crates and overturned wagons, but the ironclad's cannon quickly reduced both it and them to flaming splinters and bloody chunks.

A tumbling ricochet whistled overhead, to splash in the darkness on the farside of the yacht. McGrath turned away from the ship's rail to confront Loveless, his face a twisted mask of fury. "Why you sawed-off little sadistic *bastard*! You've betrayed us!"

Dr. Loveless merely lowered his binoculars and cocked his head. "My dear General, after donating half my physical being to the service of the Confederacy, after creating and demonstrating the original prototype of this weapon, how did you and General Lee repay *my* loyalty? You surrendered at Appomattox!" Loveless put the binoculars back to his eyes.

"So please, General, do not presume to lecture me on who has betrayed whom." Loveless studied the massacre in progress a bit longer, then made a small beckoning gesture with his right hand. Munitia stepped smartly forward, holding a pen and a stenographer's notepad. "Make a note," Loveless said. "The turret rotation needs to be accelerated." Munitia dutifully scribbled on the pad.

In the distance the rolling thunder died down to a sporadic crackling, as the light of the flare faded away. A moment later another rocket arced skyward and the butchery resumed. Men were cut in half by .50-caliber bullets and died in mid-scream.

McGrath looked to the circle of fascinated foreign faces for help, saw there was none, and acted alone. "Dr. Loveless! I *demand* that you give the order to stop this carnage!"

Loveless ignored him, and continued dictating to Munitia. "We're going to have to work on the reloading routine. I'm hearing far too much time between screams." Scribble, scribble, scribble. Munitia wrote it down.

McGrath roughly shoved her aside. "*Did you hear me, sir?*"

Loveless shook his head nonchalantly. "Yes, yes. Don't dribble in your pants, General. I heard you." He lowered the binoculars and sighed. "McGrath?" he said gently. "I spared your life tonight because you have served me well, and because I sense you are a man of vision. Please, allow me to explain." Loveless set the binoculars where his lap would have been if he'd had one, backed his wheelchair away from the rail, and turned around to address the foreign dignitaries. His back was to McGrath.

"Gentlemen," Loveless began, "since the beginning of written history, a nation's power has been determined by the size of its standing army. But tonight, that chapter draws to a close.

"My friends, the Age of Rifles is over. The traditional army—to say nothing of the United States—will soon become extinct. You have been kind enough to provide your best weapons for this exercise, and the general here has graciously supplied trained troops, and yet these two forces together could not stand five minutes against the might of a *single* land ironclad! They have been laid low by a *cripple*—as the general so aptly put it—and the power of mechinology."

Loveless paused to catch his breath and wet his lips with a sip of champagne. He failed to notice the ghastly expressions on the face of his audience or the gunfire, explosions, and screams in the distance.

"Those men ashore are not really dying," Loveless resumed. "They are being out-evolved. The future belongs to the masters of the *machine*! I ask you, envision not armies, but rather entire *fleets* of land ironclads, moving—"

Loveless felt a cold gun barrel pressed against his neck and stopped. "You have a dissenting opinion, General?"

McGrath's voice was a low and feral rasp. "For the last time, Doctor, give your people the order to desist."

Loveless sighed, and moved his hands to the wheelchair armrests. "General, I understand your distress. But believe me, those men on that field are *not* dying senselessly. It is for a far greater cause than you can begin to imagine." Unnoticed by McGrath, Loveless's right thumb moved to rest on a certain small protruding stud. "Their sacrifice will pave the way—"

McGrath thumbed back the hammer of his revolver. *"Then may you go straight to Hell, sir!"*

"After you, General." Loveless pressed the stud.

The concealed 10-gauge buckshot shells in the backs of the armrest tubes very nearly disemboweled McGrath. The revolver fell from McGrath's nerveless hand; the general stared at his ruined belly with a great and terrible expression of disbelief, then, without another word, crumpled to the deck.

Doctor Loveless only looked over his shoulder at the bloody mess, sniffed disdainfully, and shook his head. "Bloodbath McGrath, indeed." He turned to the foreign dignitaries, and for the first time saw the sick fear on their faces, as they tried to guess what other weapons his wheelchair might include.

"Well, friends," Loveless said brightly, "that concludes tonight's entertainment! We'll be docking in ten minutes. Ladies, feed him to the crabs!" Munitia and Lippenreider unceremoniously heaved McGrath's body over the rail. It hit the water with a ponderous splash.

"Now if you'll excuse me," Loveless said as he rolled away, "I've got a train to catch."

The black train waited ominously on the tracks, half a mile from Malheureux Point. Loveless's private car was not so much a coach as a riveted, armored, fortress on wheels. It also, as one of the Prussians noted, did not appear to have a locomotive.

Loveless seemed unconcerned with that detail as he led his entourage toward the car. As he wheeled up the boarding ramp he shouted to his guests, "My destination is both the future, and the past! Forget about Paul Revere: *This* will be the most revolutionary ride in the history of America!" Loveless turned his wheelchair around to watch, beaming, as the land ironclad drove up onto the railroad tracks, lowered a set of locomotive wheels, retracted its treads, and backed into the black car. Pneumatic couplers locked and hissed; with a slow, groaning noise, the two units crawled together and merged into one solid machine: black death on wheels.

Loveless wheeled himself aboard the train, then stopped in the hatchway and turned to face his guests one last time.

"If you don't want to miss the ride, have the last payment of one thousand kilograms of your country's gold in my hands no later than Friday. That's when I will be making my little proposal to President Grant, one that I am ever so confident he will find it in his heart to accept."

Loveless paused a moment, then dismissed his audience with a jaunty wave.

"My yacht will take you all back to New Orleans! For now, *au revoir*, *auf wiedersehen*, *adios*, and ta-ta!"

CHAPTER EIGHT

On a still night the sound of a rifle shot can echo for miles, and cannon fire sounds like distant thunder. Jim West checked the sky for rain clouds, saw none, and developed a pretty fair guess at what he was riding into. The shooting seemed to die down when he was still about a half mile shy of Malheureux Point, but all the same he slowed his stolen horse to a trot, shifted the reins to his left hand, and rode in cautiously, with pistol ready.

The narrow road ended in a broad meadow that looked like some particularly nasty Gothic vision of Hell. Lit by moonlight and the ruddy glow of many small dying fires, the ground was littered with spent cartridges, dead men in bloody Confederate uniforms, and the occasional still-smoldering shell crater.

Just like Cemetery Ridge after Pickett's Charge, West

noted. Then he noticed a little difference that made all the little hairs on the back of his neck snap to and stand at attention.

The meadow was silent. No moans and muttered prayers from the dying. No inhuman screams from wounded horses. No sounds at all, save for the cheery crackle of the fires, the singing of frogs and crickets, and the *clip-clop-clip* of his horses's hooves.

Then West made another discovery, and began to understand. Everywhere he looked, the soft ground was crisscrossed by a set of strange, parallel tracks, that traced in broad sweeping lines over smashed crates, crushed wagons, and twisted steel rifles.

West dismounted, tied the horse off to what remained of a shattered tree trunk, and advanced cautiously toward the center of the meadow. As he walked, he began to notice that the grass was mowed in a weird, concentric, ring pattern. In the exact center of the bull's-eye he found a headless corpse in a colonel's uniform. The man's pistol was still in its holster. West knelt and checked the gun.

It was fully loaded and unfired. It was also noticeably nicer than the revolver West had lifted off George back at the Loveless mansion. West hesitated a moment, then decided Ichabod Crane there wouldn't mind, and slipped the revolver into his left holster. West stood up.

He's got to be here. West began walking around the meadow, poking and kicking corpses. *These are his men. That homicidal bastard* must *be here.* He spotted one body that looked like a beached whale, and with some effort heaved it over. Half the man's face was gone, but he

clearly had an intact left ear. *Not McGrath. Where* is *he?*
West spotted another familiar-looking body in a pile of
wreckage; a faded corporal's chevron on a gray sleeve;
the letters *T H U G* tattooed on the knuckles of the right
hand. West grabbed the arm and pulled. It was not at-
tached.

"He's dead, Jim," a voice behind him said. West
dropped the severed arm and spun into a draw.

Artemus Gordon was standing there, stroking his chin,
obviously fascinated by the horror all around. West uncocked the pistol and slipped it back into his holster. Gordon turned to help Rita down from the carriage.

Once she was safely on the ground, Gordon began
strolling toward the center of the meadow, all the while
talking, pointing, and gesturing broadly. "Whatever it
was, it obviously came up out of the swamp, *there*. From
the way these corpses are positioned, it must have laid
down a 360-degree pattern of fire, then moved off . . .
that way?" Gordon pointed inland. He stopped walking,
rested his foot on the colonel's corpse, and scratched his
chin. "My God, what kind of weapon can it be?" He
looked at Rita as if asking her.

"Excuse me," she replied. "I'm going to throw up."
She ducked behind the wagon and gagged audibly.

West walked over and handed Gordon the revolver
he'd picked up. "This is Colonel Ottoman's pistol." Gordon abruptly noticed what he was using for a footrest and
stepped back. "It was unfired and holstered. Whoever did
this, these poor dumb crackers thought they were meeting friends."

Gordon nodded and handed the gun back to West. "Any ideas, who or what?"

"Yeah." West looked at the strange tracks in the soft ground and got a faraway look in his eyes. "It's a machine; a big metal machine. It just rolls on and on; makes a kind of a screeching sound, like a wounded animal. It's got a turret on top, like a *Monitor*, and it swivels from side to side like an eagle's head and shoots all over."

Gordon's eyes widened. "You saw it?"

West shook his head. "Didn't have to. I've heard about it. But I thought it was just crazy survivors' stories."

Gordon blinked. "Er, James—what survivors? There are no survivors here."

"Not here." West turned away from Gordon, drew a deep breath, and let it out in a heavy sigh. "Ever hear of New Liberty? It was a freed slave town, up in south Illinois. Good country. Peach orchards. Farmland." West shook his head.

"Just before the war ended—in early spring, 1865— there were a lot of Confederate raiders running loose in Missouri and Kentucky. Irregulars; crazy men. Guys like William Quantrill, the James brothers, and Bloody Bill Anderson. Rebs who were never gonna surrender, no matter what Robert E. Lee did. Quantrill alone murdered more than 150 people in Lawrence, Kansas, and he was one of the sane ones.

"Well, in late March of '65 the army got word that Quantrill was helping a Reb general—a guy named *Mc-Grath*—plan a raid across the river, on New Liberty.

Since it was a freed slave town, they ordered the 9th Negro Cavalry in to defend it."

West turned back to Gordon, with a terrible haunted look in his eyes. "We got there a day too late," he said softly. "Old men, women, children: McGrath used 'em for target practice. The survivors—and there weren't many of 'em—said the Rebs had a crazy machine; a *Monitor* gunboat that climbed right up out of the Big Muddy and blew the town to Hell and gone. Made a horrible, screeching sound."

Gordon's expression became one of utter fascination. "A land ironclad, you say? Incredible!" He turned and pointed to where the strange parallel tracks led off into the darkness. "Do you think it's still around here?"

"Well, it ain't shooting at us, so I'd say not. There's a railroad track about a quarter mile off that way. I'm guessing they loaded it on a flatcar and hauled it away."

A clear, loud, and ghoulishly miserable moan came to them through the night. Gordon became concerned. "Rita?"

West grabbed Gordon by the shoulder and steered him in the other direction. "No, that came from the marsh. Come on!"

McGrath opened his eyes again, and to his considerable surprise found that he was not yet dead. Freezing cold, paralyzed, and in agony, yes, but not *quite* dead. He let his eyes fall shut. Involuntarily, another moan escaped his lips.

He heard voices, as if through cotton. He searched for

his last reserves of life energy, found them, and opened his eyes.

Jim West's homely, jug-eared face was hovering over him.

McGrath began to reconsider his position. Perhaps he was dead after all, and this was Hell. He hoped not. He hated to think that Jim West was the devil who'd be tormenting him for all eternity. Another face drifted into view, next to West; a man he didn't recognize. It made no sense. Why would the Devil have assigned *two* personal demons to McGrath?

Then the third face floated into view—a beautiful, brown-eyed angel—and McGrath managed a weak smile. No, he was definitely not dead, and the question of his eternal forwarding address was not entirely settled. He licked his lips and tried to form dying thoughts into words. His voice, when it emerged, was a hoarse and ragged whisper.

"What's the matter, West?" McGrath taunted. "Thought you'd be happy to find me . . . like this."

West glared. "I was hoping to kill you myself."

The angel frowned. "*That*'s a nice way to talk to people."

McGrath managed a laugh, that turned into a choked cough. "Well you'll just have to learn to live with it. As I've lived all these years with the blame . . . for New Liberty." The effort tired McGrath. He closed his eyes.

Something lifted and shook him. He could barely feel it. "*What do you mean?*" an angry voice demanded.

McGrath responded to the demand and opened his

eyes one last time. "Loveless . . . his plan. He drove the machine that night. Pulled the triggers. I didn't know what he had in mind. Cannon breech blew out; damn near killed him.

"He's smarter now. Left the dirty work to others, here." McGrath suddenly found his eyelids impossibly heavy and let them fall closed. He felt rough hands upon his collar, shaking him.

"Where is *he? Why did he do this? Where did Loveless go?"*

But McGrath found that he no longer cared. Life, death, North, South; none of it mattered anymore. He was flying through the air, arcing towards the surface of a deep, dark pool. He was twelve years old again, and at his favorite swimming hole.

"I know," he heard the brown-eyed angel say.

Of course you do, McGrath thought.

Splashdown . . .

West let McGrath's lifeless body plop back into the mud and reeds. He turned to Rita. *"Huh?"*

"I know where Loveless is going," Rita insisted.

"And how would you happen to know that?"

"Amazonia, Munitia, Lippenreider—" Rita realized the names weren't registering, and tried again. "Loveless's women. They talk. 'What's it going to be like in Utah?' " Rita said, imitating someone. " 'Can you get a drink there?' " She shifted her voice down a key and into a Germanic accent. "'I vonder if my hair vill get frizzy in zis Shpyder Canyon?' '*Mais oui*, and what is so especial about this *Promontory Point*?' "

West's jaw dropped. "Omigod. He's gonna kill Grant."

Gordon grabbed West by the sleeve and dragged him into motion. "C'mon, Jim. Help me get that horse of yours hitched up to the carriage."

Coleman was relaxing with an issue of the Montgomery-Ward ladies' foundation catalog when West and Gordon rushed aboard the *Wanderer.* "Get this train movin'!" West barked. "What's the fastest track to Utah?"

The engineer stubbed out his cigarette, folded the magazine, set it aside, and got to his feet. "The fastest track is also the only track, Captain West: the Union Pacific. But may I remind you that No. 5 is a *locomotive*, not a horse? You can't just leap on its back, kick it in the pistons, shout *yee-haw*! and gallop off. It'll take me at least thirty minutes to stoke the boiler, bring up steam pressure, get the yard crew to switch us onto the main line—"

Gordon cut in. "Coleman? There is a homicidal madman with a gun and a grudge on his way to Utah to meet President Grant."

"—but since we don't have thirty minutes, I'll do it in five," the engineer finished. He turned and dashed forward to start firing up the engine.

West moved over to the pool table; Gordon to the Victrola. Both of them paused a long moment to look out the window at Rita, who was standing in the railyard below, shivering in her thin camisole and gazing up at the train like a sad puppy.

"I still don't see why we couldn't have given her a ride back to Texas," Gordon said wistfully. "It is on the way."

West shot him a hard look. "On the way to stopping a *madman*! Is that any place for an 'entertainer'? We got the president to think about! I know this Spider Canyon; it's just twenty-five miles from Promontory Point!"

Gordon shrugged. "We wouldn't even have known Loveless was going there if it wasn't for her. Leaving her behind seems a bit . . . ungracious. And we've got the room."

West shook his head. "Look, that kind of woman ain't gonna have any trouble raising the money for a train ticket or finding some other chump to drive her around."

Gordon pouted. "You're only being intractable because 'that kind of woman' likes me better."

"Of course she does. You two are the same dress size."

Gordon bit back his retort and conceded the verbal volley to West. The engine whistle blew. Couplers rattled and shook out, pistons chuffed, and like a twelve-ton steel inchworm with a clanging brass bell, the *Wanderer* slowly lurched into forward motion. Gordon spared another glance out the side window, but if Rita was still out there, she was hidden by the clouds of steam.

With a quiet inward sigh, Gordon turned his attention to the windup Victrola and punched a certain button on its side. The turntable deck flipped over, to reveal a telegraph key and receiver. He switched on the gravity batteries, gave them a moment to warm up, and began to tap out *CQ, CQ*.

West, meanwhile, was circling the pool table, punching and poking every promising-looking stud and projection. On the second lap, he started kicking things, too.

"Cue rack," Gordon said, not looking up.

"Huh?"

"The switch to flip the pool table over is on the underside of the cue rack, at the right end." Gordon continued tapping.

"I knew that," West said. Nonchalantly, he continued to stroll around the table, until he just happened to be standing near the cue rack. After one more sidelong glance to see if Gordon was watching him, West hit the button. The pool table revolved into the floor, and in its place stood a rack loaded with state-of-the-art weapons.

West whistled soft and low.

"Is there some problem?" Gordon asked, as he looked up from the telegraph.

West kind of smiled, kind of shrugged, kind of frowned, and kicked the carpet. "Uh—that lynch mob at Loveless's house. They took my guns. I managed to grab these two"—West pulled George's and the headless colonel's pistols from his holsters and laid them on the side table—"but I was really hoping we had a pair of Colt Army .44s here."

Gordon turned back to the telegraph and resumed tapping. "Other side."

West stepped around to the other side of the rack and found a battery of nickel-plated revolvers. He lifted one.

It had a solid topstrap like a Remington, a frame-mounted loading gate like a Richards, and the grip and lockwork of a Colt. It seemed a touch on the heavy side, but otherwise felt *good* in his hand.

"Advanced prototype," Gordon said, answering the question before West asked it. "New gun Colt is developing for the army. Forty-*five* caliber; they call it the Peacemaker. Makes your old .44 look like a popgun. You'll find the cartridges down and to the right." West looked in the indicated place and found an unmarked pasteboard box that proved to be full of thumb-sized cartridges. He whistled again.

"I'm glad you're impressed," Gordon said. "Now if you will look in the center of the rack—"

"Yeah, I recognize it," West snapped. "Allin-Springfield .50-70 carbine. Cavalry's had them for three years, Gordon."

"Wrong. That's a *.45*-70. New experimental cartridge; same powder charge, much higher chamber pressure, greater velocity and range than the fifty. That gun will drop a charging buffalo in its tracks at a quarter mile."

West flipped the breech shut, put the rifle to his shoulder, and squeezed off an imaginary shot. "I'll remember that if we're ever attacked by charging buffalo." He put the rifle back on the rack and came around to Gordon's side.

"Now on this side—" Gordon continued.

West arched an eyebrow at the selection of lever-action rifles and carbines. "I suppose you're going to tell me these are not Henry rifles." He hefted one, cracked the action open, and examined the inside of the receiver.

"Not exactly. It's Henry's design, but Oliver Winchester owns the factory now. Therefore what you are holding is an advanced prototype Winchester rifle in caliber .44 Winchester Center Fire."

"The man do like the sound of his own name." West closed the rifle's action, put it to his shoulder, and was well pleased. Setting the rifle aside, he rooted around the gun rack until he found a box clearly marked with the word *Winchester* in big red letters. He dumped out a handful of the thumb-sized cartridges.

West did a double take, then compared the Colt revolver cartridge side by side to the almost identical Winchester rifle cartridge. "You can't swap 'em, can you?" Gordon looked up from his telegraphing long enough to shake his head, but he seemed to be getting testy about the interruptions. "You know," West said, "Colt and Winchester could save everybody a lot of trouble if they'd just use the same load."

"Why don't you send them a telegram?" Gordon snapped. "I will be done in another minute, if we can just avoid any more *interrup*—"

West slipped a cartridge into the rifle, then looked over Gordon's shoulders. "What're you doin'?"

Gordon punctuated a string of code with an angry slap on the telegraph key. "I am *trying* to send a telegram to Fort Logan in Utah! I thought it *might* be prudent to apprise President Grant that a murderous lunatic is heading his way with—"

West shook his head. "Yeah, well, you can apprise 'til your fingers fall off, but it ain't gonna do any good." West nodded out the window. "Look." Gordon looked where West directed. The train was up to speed and moving quite fast now, as judged by the speed with which the line of telegraph poles—

Correction. The line of shattered, splintered, and blasted remains of telegraph poles—was racing past the window. Some of the stumps of poles were still burning.

Gordon sat back, stroked his chin, and considered the now-useless telegraph key. "You know, I've been trying to put myself in Loveless's shoes—"

West snorted. "Good luck on that one."

"My point is, if this is strictly a matter of personal vengeance against Grant, why are the ministers of France, England, and Spain interested?" A small bell chimed in the galley. Gordon got up and walked around the partition.

West shrugged. "They like a good party?"

Gordon returned, this time wearing a white chef's jacket and carrying a steaming pot. "*Epaule de Chevreuil Farcie!*" he announced proudly, as he set the dish down on the dining table. West stared at the bubbling pot with obvious misgivings.

"Stuffed shoulder of venison," Gordon translated. "Cooked in a daubiere—a clay pot."

West rolled his eyes. "*That* is what you do on a mission? You *cook?*"

This time it was Gordon's turn to shrug. "Fine. Don't eat it." He sat down, tucked a linen napkin under his chin, and dished himself a portion. Just as Gordon was about to put a forkful in his mouth, he heard a faint *tap, tap, tap* at the back door of the coach.

Gordon looked to West. They made silent eye contact, and for the first time, they both seemed to be on the same track. West drew one of his new revolvers and eased toward the door. Gordon stood and quietly, silently, worked around to the other side of the door. West got ready, then nodded to Gordon. Gordon yanked the door open.

Rita was standing on the rear platform of the car, hair whipping in the slipstream wind, arms wrapped around herself, lips a lovely shade of blue. "Hi," she said, smiling wanly. "It's, uh, kinda chilly out here tonight."

West marched Rita into the car and sat her down at the dinner table. "What the *Hell* are you doing, sneaking on our train like this?"

Rita sniffed. "Well, if you two'd been gentlemen and offered me a ride, I wouldn't have had to!" She looked at the food spread out on the table, and her eyes widened. "Say, are you going to eat all that? I'm starving." Without waiting for an answer, she grabbed a plate and started dishing up. West could only shake his head.

"Make yourself a sandwich," he suggested. "And take it with you when you get off. Your free ride is over."

"But I can *help* you," Rita said, around a mouthful of meat.

West was dubious. "How can you possibly do that?"

She swallowed the food and chased it with a gulp of wine. "Well, while I was standing out there, I heard you wondering why all those foreign guys were at Loveless's party. You want me to tell you?"

This got Gordon's interest. "By all means, do."

Rita stuffed another forkful in her mouth. "They're here to get their land back." She chewed, then slowed down enough to start tasting. "This is fantastic!" she said to Gordon. "You can cut it with a fork! How did you cook this?"

Gordon fairly beamed. "Well, in a daubiere—a clay pot. It's a French method which involves—"

West clamped his hand over Gordon's mouth. "*What* land?"

Rita swallowed again, then considered her reply. "Let's see, they kept arguing about who rightfully owns Nueva York. Then I heard Loveless say something about how the Louisiana Purchase was a real bad deal for Queen . . . somebody of France."

"Spain," Gordon corrected. "Queen Isabella of Spain."

Rita shrugged. "Whatever."

"This is crazy," West said. "We bought Louisiana from Napoleon. She doesn't know what she's talking about." He stepped over to the speaker tube and whistled for the engineer. "Coleman! Stop the train!" Immediately the car shuddered, and there came the sound of hissing pneumatic brakes as the train began to slow.

Rita dropped her fork. "Wait!" West and Gordon both turned and looked at her. "I . . . uh, I'm afraid I haven't been completely honest with you."

West snorted. "No, really?"

"I, ah, didn't really go to New Orleans to become one of Loveless's women."

Gordon had assumed his usual posture of standing there with his arms crossed, looking highly intelligent. "So you're not really an entertainer then, either."

She shook her head. "No. My name is Rita Escobar. I went to New Orleans to find Guillermo Escobar. He's . . . my father."

Gordon's eyes popped. "Of course! Professor Escobar, Ph.D. in hydraulics! I was looking for him, too!"

With this revelation, West's attitude changed. He nodded to Rita. "Sorry if you had the wrong guy working on your case, Señorita Escobar. But don't worry: If your father is still alive, I'll find him and send him home." With those words the train came to a complete stop, and Coleman entered the car.

"Miss Escobar is getting off," West explained.

Coleman looked at Rita, then Gordon, then back to West. "We can't put this poor young woman off the train! We're in the middle of nowhere!" Rita smiled sweetly at Coleman.

West felt his resolve being undermined.

Rita took a step closer to West and *looked* at him with her big, beautiful, brown eyes. "Please, Jim. He's the only family I have left. What am I supposed to do, sit at home and wait to hear whether he's been killed? If he was your father, what would you do?"

West felt his resolve collapsing like a levee in a spring flood. "Look, lady, I got nothing personal against you. It's just that—what happens when we catch up with

Loveless, with you on the train? You were lucky to get away from him once."

Impulsively, Rita grabbed West's hand, and West felt the rest of his resolve vanish. "I know you'd never let him take me back, Jim. And I've seen how you can shoot." In spite of himself, West smiled.

Gordon stepped forward, perhaps a bit too intrusively. "I assure you, Miss Escobar, an attack by Loveless would be an exercise in futility. Allow me to show you." He raised his hands, as if leading a tour group. "I designed the *Wanderer* for comfort, functionality—"

He pressed a stud and a bookcase dropped to reveal a gun port. "—and imperviousness to attack."

West drew his shiny new Peacemakers, twirled them, and reholstered them. *Damn, these guns balance nice!*

"I'm the impervious part," West explained.

Gordon chuckled. "Hardly. This train is *completely* armor-plated." He rapped on the flocked walls for emphasis, and they rang with a metallic sound. "Heavily armed." He pressed another button, and a wall-mounted lamp transformed into the firing mechanism of a Gatling gun. "And if, by some inconceivable fluke, they did manage to gain entrance—" He stepped over to the cue rack and pressed the stud to return the pool table to its normal state, then plucked the six ball out of the side pocket.

"An innocent billiard ball this way." Gordon thumbed the numbered dot. It sank into the surface of the ball with a click. "But depress the number and it becomes a sleeping-gas bomb, effective in under three seconds!"

Gordon unclicked the bomb and triumphantly rolled it into the corner pocket.

"So rest assured, Miss, you are *completely* safe within these four walls." Gordon smiled at Rita, broadly.

West could only shake his head and try not to laugh. It'd been years since he'd watched a man try so hard to impress a girl who was so obviously not interested.

He wiped the smirk off his face, and spoke. "I don't know about you, ma'am, but I know I'll sleep a whole lot better tonight, knowing we're ready . . . in case Loveless breaks in and challenges Arte to a game of pool." West yawned.

Rita picked up the cue and managed a polite little ladylike yawn herself. "Speaking of that, I'm awfully tired. Artemus, do you think I could borrow something to sleep in?"

West jumped in before Gordon could answer. "*I* got something you can use. Ain't stylish, but it's practical . . ."

Coleman had returned to the locomotive and gotten the train under way again. Gordon dimmed the lamp over the table, then settled in on the davenport.

West glared at him from the other sofa. "Hey, Arte," he said. "Refresh my memory. When exactly did we say she could have the bedroom?"

Gordon stroked his chin. "Now that you mention it, I don't recall that we did."

The door to the stateroom slid open. West and Gordon looked up; Rita was standing in the doorway, shyly clinging to a doorjamb, half-revealing herself in one of West's red union suits. "Well, good night, gentlemen," she said sweetly, "and thank you for saving me."

"*My pleasure*," Gordon and West said simultaneously.

Rita turned to go back into the stateroom. Either she'd forgotten about or failed to fasten securely the buttons on the back flap of the union suit, for it was open, exposing her nicely shaped derrière for all to see.

West nearly choked. "Uh, Rita—"

She stopped in the doorway and looked back over her shoulder at West. "Yes, Jim?"

"Uh, hope it's not too breezy back there for you."

She shook her head. "Actually it looks very cozy, Jim." She resumed moving.

"Rita?" Gordon asked. She stopped again, and this time looked back over her other shoulder at Artemus.

"If there's anything you need . . . anything at all . . . you'll let me know?"

She smiled. "Of course, Arte. Well, sweet dreams." She blew them both a kiss and closed the door.

West and Gordon stayed awake for *hours*, each man keeping a jealous eye on the other. . . .

CHAPTER NINE

The *Wanderer* burrowed through the night, pistons hammering, smokestack flaming. Coleman stayed at the throttle of No. 5 and catnapped when he could, in the long stretches between the spur-line junctions and the tank towns. A steam engine lives on coal, water, and grease: he had to stop to lube and fuel in Shreveport, and again in Wichita Falls, but according to the dispatchers in those towns he was closing the gap on a strange black locomotive that was running without lights or signals, and he had the highball all the way through to Denver.

Halfway to Amarillo, the sun came up in the east like a big bald giant peeking out over the edge of Oklahoma. Coleman threw another few shovels full of coal into the firebox, slammed the door shut with the shovel, and cast an experienced eye at the gauges. Running all night at full throttle was not doing No. 5 any good, and Coleman worried about his pet engine. She was definitely going to need her flues cleaned soon, and was probably in line for a set of new tie-rod bearings when this sprint was over. But that would have to wait until Denver at least, or more likely, Salt Lake City.

His worries about the locomotive allayed for the moment, Coleman leaned out the cab window and tried to see what the dawn's early light revealed. The track ahead curved gently to the left for the next few miles.

Coleman blinked, wiped the soot from his goggles, and looked again. The *Wanderer* apparently had made good time since Wichita Falls, was now running about half a mile behind a strange, black, articulated locomotive. He grabbed the speaking tube. "West! Gordon! Gentlemen, wake up! We have Loveless off the port bow, nine hundred yards and closing!"

Lippenreider lowered her binoculars and turned to Dr. Loveless. "It's West. And someone named Gordon."

Loveless shook his head in wryly amused amazement. "Miss East must have failed. What a pity." He rotated his wheelchair like a turret. "*Munitia! Amazonia!* Let's prepare a suitable welcome for our persistent friend!"

At Coleman's word, West and Gordon leapt out of their makeshift beds and threw on their clothes. West immediately ran to the weapons rack and began loading guns. Gordon tidied up the place a bit, set out a plate of scones, and starting brewing a pot of coffee. Rita emerged from the stateroom, still wearing West's red union suit, her hair a beautiful, wild, Cindy Crawford–type mess. "What's going on?" Rita asked nervously.

Gordon ushered her back into the stateroom, fighting the overwhelming temptation to hurry her along with a little swat on her still-bare buttocks. "Get back in there! Take cover! And for God's sake, get some clothes on!"

Meanwhile West had finished loading everything that could be loaded, and went back to the sofa to finish getting dressed. He sat down and pulled his right boot on. A shiny three-inch steel stiletto popped out of the toe.

"What the Hell*?"*

Gordon turned from his shaving mirror. "I took the liberty of installing it while you were sleeping. I don't just *cook* while I'm on a mission."

"You leave my damn boots alone!" West stared at the knife and wiggled his toes inside his boot, thumping his heel on the floor, until he figured out how to retract the blade. Then he inspected his left boot very carefully before pulling it on.

In the next half hour the *Wanderer* gained perhaps two hundred yards on the black engine, and the plains they were passing across gave way to mountain foothills. West grabbed Gordon's "quarter-mile" rifle and a box of shells, went forward to the locomotive cab, and got on Coleman's nerves. *"Come on, man, can't you get any more speed out of this tub?"*

Coleman tweaked the throttle slightly and winced as the needle on a large gauge crept closer to the red line.

"I'm giving you all she's got, Captain. She cannah take much more o' this!"

West grabbed on to his cowboy hat, leaned out the window, and tried to guess whether there was any point in risking a shot. The track ahead curved to the right, and about a mile and a half ahead it went into a tunnel.

"Can we catch them in the tunnel?" West shouted at Coleman over the wind noise.

"Do we *want* to?" Coleman shouted right back.

The black train plunged into the mountain tunnel. Militia switched on an electric reading lamp and spread the map out before Dr. Loveless. "There's a parallel siding just past the other end of this tunnel," she pointed out. "We can throw the switch by remote, then throw it back after we've cleared the switch. We'll have to slow down to make the turn."

Loveless rubbed his hands together and grinned like a skull. "*Ex*cellent!"

The *Wanderer* erupted from the tunnel. West leaned out the window again and peered ahead, squinting at the bright daylight. The black train had disappeared! "*What the—?*"

With a deafening clang, a heavy lead bullet splattered off the steel side of the locomotive, inches from West's head. West dived for cover and met Coleman on the deck. More bullets followed in quick succession, this time accompanied by the unmistakable staccato chatter of a

Artemus Gordon (Kevin Kline) demonstrates an intriguing scientific invention to James West (Will Smith) that will help the pair determine the whereabouts of the nefarious Dr. Loveless (Kenneth Branagh).

Miss Lippenreider (Sofia Eng) employs her skill at reading lips for the evil genius Dr. Arliss Loveless (Kenneth Branagh).

Rita Escobar (Salma Hayek) does a turn as a saloon girl.

The town of Silverado is bombed by Loveless's war machine, the Tarantula.

The battle-worn General McGrath (Ted Levine) and his hearing aid.

Collared! Artemus Gordon and James West at the mercy of Arliss Loveless.

James West views the carnage after Loveless's attack on Malheureux Point.

Loveless's Lovelies: Munitia (Musetta Vander), Amazonia (Frederique van der Wal), and Lippenreider.

Loveless announces his plans for restructuring
the United States.

James West climbs one leg of Loveless's gigantic war machine
in a desperate race to save President Ulysses S. Grant.

Fire when ready: the lovely Munitia with one of Loveless's fearsome inventions, the disk launcher.

heavy Gatling gun. The wooden top and glass side curtains of the locomotive cab shattered and splintered, as hot lead spatters stung West's face and hands and ricochets whistled past his ears.

Coleman seemed to be okay. West crawled around the deck like a turtle, found some cover, and peeked out. Loveless's train was now running beside them, on a parallel track about a hundred yards off, and the big blonde woman was standing in some kind of ring turret at the stern, hands on the cranks of a pair of Gatling guns. She spotted West at the same time as he saw her and swung the guns around.

West dived for what little cover he could find, curled up in a ball, and wished that the *Wanderer* had a cannon.

Dr. Loveless sat on the observation deck of his train, sipping an iced lemonade and watching the *Wanderer* through opera glasses. Amazonia let up firing long enough to reload.

Loveless laughed. "Amazonia, my dear, I believe that we have disabused Captain West of the notion that one's problems are solved when one sees the light at the end of the tunnel!"

Amazonia finished reloading the guns and slapped the actions closed. "He's gotten into a well-protected corner. Shall I wait for him to stick his head out like a prairie dog again?"

Loveless considered the option. "No, we'll kill him soon enough. Why don't you shoot the rest of his train some more?" Amazonia nodded, smiled, cranked up the

Gatlings, and resumed raking the *Wanderer* from stem to stern.

Rita screamed like a steam whistle as .50-caliber bullets ripped through the side of the stateroom. Window glass, china cups, and splattered bits of scones flew through the air in a remarkably messy maelstrom of destruction. West seized the opportunity to leap out of the locomotive, dash across the top of the tender, then burst into the parlor car and throw himself on top of Rita, to shield her very tightly with his body.

Gordon shook his head. "Aren't you overreacting a bit?" He lifted the speaking tube. "Coleman! Raise the shields!" Within seconds great steel plates had clanged shut over the windows of the car, rendering it dark and messy, but safe. Amazonia's Gatlings might as well have been twin peashooters for all the effect her bullets now had.

Gordon indulged himself with another smug moment. "God, I love this train!"

West reluctantly disentangled himself from Rita, then hit the button that transformed the lamp into a Gatling gun. Locking the gun into position on the firing port, he slapped in a loaded magazine and began to return fire.

"Gordon!" West shouted, between bursts. "You still got that little notepad thing?"

Gordon flicked his wrists just so and an instant later was holding a pen and notepad. "Yes?"

"Write this down! 'Put. A. God. Damn. *Cannon*, on this train!' Got that?!"

Gordon scribbled. Rita looked over his shoulder at his wrist gizmos. "You know," she suggested, "you could put a gun and a knife on those."

Gordon winced. "Not you, *too*?" He retracted the pen and notepad and moved to peer out a firing port. "Hey! They're slowing down!" West stopped firing, went to the back door of the car, and opened it. The *Wanderer* raced past the point where the siding rejoined the main track. As if by itself, the switch threw, then Loveless's black train crossed onto the main track behind the *Wanderer* and began accelerating.

"Uh-oh," West said.

"Now why would they want to do that?" Gordon wondered aloud.

West pushed Gordon inside and slammed the door. A deafening blast rattled the china, and the *Wanderer* careened wildly as a shell exploded to their right. A second blast followed moments later, and the exploding shell burst to their left.

"'Cause they couldn't shoot their cannon at us from the *front!*" West shouted. "Any more questions?"

Gordon shook his head. "Only solutions." He reached over to the cabin wall and flipped a lever. Thick steam clouds began pouring from the rear of the car. Within seconds the black train was completely lost in the thick, artificial fog. The cannon fire stopped.

"Cute," West said. "Long as they don't figure out we're still straight ahead of them on the tracks. Does give me an idea, though." He grabbed a coil of rope and lay down on the pool table. "Would it put you out too much

to hit the button, then get on the winch?" Gordon
shrugged, and hit the button. The pool table rotated into
the floor. Rita gasped in surprise.

"I taught him how it worked," Gordon said to her.

On the underside of the car, head inches above the bal-
last and railroad ties speeding by, West hand-over-handed
himself back to the winch, pulled the cable loose, and at-
tached it to the eye-hook on the mechanic's creeper. Then
he crawled onto the creeper, rolled over onto his back,
and slapped the release lever. The creeper dropped onto
the tracks, the small steel wheels locked into place on the
insides of the rails, and the elevator cables released themselves.

Brilliant!" muttered Gordon, in reluctant admiration.
He donned a pair of thick leather gloves, opened a hatch
in the floor, and raised the winch to operating position.
"Unorthodox, but inspired!" With one hand on the cable
and the other on the winch handle, he began to crank it,
slowly paying out cable.

"What's brilliant?" Rita asked.

"I'd intended the mechanic's creeper to be used for
working on the undersides of the trucks while the train is
standing still. It never occurred to me that one could also
use it while the train is *moving*."

The creeper, with West aboard, emerged from under
the rear platform of the car, dangling from the end of the

taut winch cable like a heavy fish on a long line. West gave Gordon a thumbs-up, and Gordon continued.

Suddenly, *ping!* A tooth flew off a bronze gear. The trolley lurched a foot. *Pop!* Another tooth sheared off, and the trolley jumped again. West began to feel apprehensive.

Ccrruncchhhhgriiinndsqueeeeeeeeaaalll!

Gordon jumped back as the winch destroyed itself. The cable snapped taut for a moment, then parted with a *twang!* that sent the steel wire flying through the cabin like a razor-sharp whip. Rita gasped. Gordon cringed.

Jim West suddenly realized that he had just entered a whole new world of hurt.

The trolley slowed. The locomotive didn't. Loveless's onrushing black train bore down on West like—well, like an onrushing black train. West sucked in his gut, held his breath, visualized himself as a flapjack, and personally apologized to God for every extra slice of sweet potato pie he'd ever had in his entire life.

Apparently it worked. The leading edge of the locomotive sheared two buttons off his jacket, but no important parts off his body. *Okay Jim, not exactly the way you planned it, but it'll do.* West sprang into action, throwing a loop of rope around a convenient projection on the underside of the trailing car. The rope held for half a second. . . .

Then slowly, like a piece of saltwater taffy, began to s-t-r-e-t-c-h—

Oh no, not another *stupid rope trick! ARTEMUS!*

* * *

Panting, swearing, and wild-eyed, West pulled himself up onto the stern platform of Loveless's train. No one was guarding the rear entrance, which was what West was counting on. He took a moment to catch his breath, then climbed up onto the roof of the train and headed for the locomotive.

Locomotive runs on steam, he thought it through again. *Piston cylinders are down by the wheels, but the cylinder exhaust vents out the stack. That's what makes 'em go* choo-choo.

You block the cylinder exhaust vent, and you've got one dead locomotive. Instantly. The only problem was, the plan called for climbing out on the top of the boiler, all the way forward to the funnel.

To his considerable surprise, West made it. *Now to plug the valve.* He tried to do it with a bandanna, first, and just got scalded for his trouble. *What else can I use?*

Another moment later he was too busy to consider the question, because someone had jumped him from behind and thrown a rawhide thong around his neck.

"The smoke screen is dissipating," Munitia reported as she bent over and squinted through the cannon's sights. "I have a clear view now. Shall I fire?"

Loveless, who was enjoying his own clear view of Munitia's transom, pursed his lips. "Can you do it without moving?"

"I'll try, sir." She squeezed the trigger—unfortunately,

just at the exact moment Loveless chose to squeeze her left buttock. As a result the shot went way high and exploded on the tracks some four hundred yards ahead of the *Wanderer.*

Coleman saw the blast and slammed on the pneumatic brakes, locking up the wheels. In a shower of sparks and accompanied by the shrill scream of bare steel on bare steel, the *Wanderer* slid inexorably toward the gaping hole in the torn-up tracks.

Back in the parlor car, Gordon and Rita went flying. . . .

West and his attacker rolled precariously atop the roaring locomotive. Whoever the man was, he was tough, and his grip on the rawhide thong never eased up for a second. West was starting to see blue spots from anoxia, and his vision was turning into a dark tunnel. *You're blacking out, Jim! Only seconds left!* He clawed desperately at the thong, trying to think of *anything.* His feet flailed spastically.

His right bootheel hit something just right. The three-inch steel stiletto popped out of the toe. West twisted into a reverse and kicked his attacker hard in the belly, unseaming him from navel to breastbone.

The man's hands went limp. West booted the dying thug off the train, ripped the thong from his neck, and gasped for air. Then he tore off his jacket, wadded it into a ball, and used it to plug the steam exhaust valve.

*   *   *

Loveless sniffed, and turned to Munitia. "Smoke?"

"I smell it, too," Lippenreider offered.

A gaslight flashed over Loveless's head. "*Amazonia! Close the blast door!*" She slammed and dogged the heavy steel hatch, a moment before the land ironclad's unvented boiler exploded and sent a massive fireball blasting through the back of the train, killing all except the four in the cannon turret.

*H*ot damn! West thought, as he picked himself up off the ground. *I figured that'd just blow out the pistons!*

Rita cowered in the shuttered and dark parlor car. "I won't let Loveless take me again! I'd rather be dead!"

Gordon wrapped his arms around her. "That's not a good thing to wish for." Outside the car they both clearly heard footsteps, approaching on the gravel railbed.

Rita grabbed a pool ball and covered the number dot with her thumb. "Please, Artemus. Don't leave me!"

"I won't. I promise. Come on." He led her into the stateroom, locking the door behind him. "On the bed. The mattress may offer some protection."

The footsteps came up the back stairs of the car, and entered the parlor. Gordon put a finger to his lips and gestured for Rita to remain still.

The footsteps halted outside the stateroom door.

The brass door handle jiggled.

"Open up," a strange, guttural voice said. "It's me, Jim."

Rita blanched. "It's a trick. I *know* Loveless!" She thumbed the detonator on the ball.

Gordon grabbed for the ball. "Rita, wait! It's—" She tried to snatch the ball back from Gordon. They bobbled it. It rolled off the edge of the bed and clunked hard on the floor.

A key clicked in the lock, and the door swung open. West was standing there, rubbing the raw welt on his neck. He smirked when he saw Gordon and Rita on the bed. *Why, Arte, you old hound! Here I am out risking my neck, and you're still trying to get Rita into bed!* Then he noticed the pool ball on the floor, spewing a cloud of purple gas.

"Oh, prairie shit," West croaked.

Blackout.

CHAPTER TEN

The afternoon sun was hot as a blacksmith's forge. Jim West dreamed that he was a piece of wrought iron, and that a cackling, demented dwarf with wheels instead of legs had dragged him out of the fire with tongs, laid him across a cold anvil, and was now busily pounding his helpless red-hot body into an endless string of black-iron horseshoes.

West opened his eyes, just a slit. He was lying flat on his back, on bare dirt, looking up at a cloudless blue sky. The sun was painfully brilliant. At the fringes of his peripheral vision, amber waves of grain swayed gently in the soft breeze. Somewhere nearby, unseen birds were singing.

His mouth felt like he had just smoked the entire annual tobacco production of the state of Tennessee.

West blinked, coughed, licked his parched lips, and

tried to think. From the shadow world of his dream, the voice of the cackling, demented dwarf taunted him again. "Welcome back to the land of the living, Captain West! Please be assured that my staff and I will take great pains to see that the remainder of your short stay here is as unpleasant as possible!"

Loveless.

West's eyes snapped open and he rolled over. Gordon was lying on the grass next to him, still unconscious, and wearing a complicated metal collar just like the one they'd taken off Professor Morton's severed head.

West gulped, and put a hand to his own throat. He was wearing an identical collar. He reached over and nudged Gordon. Gordon stirred.

" 'An innocent billiard ball this way . . .' " West said, mimicking Gordon as sarcastically as humanly possible.

Gordon sat up and rubbed his throbbing temples, as if to squeeze his pounding brains back into place. West stood and offered Gordon a hand up. They looked around. They were standing in the middle of a lush green grainfield, in the middle of, apparently, nowhere. A small wire fence, about ten feet in diameter and a foot and a half high, encircled them. The *Wanderer* rested on the tracks perhaps fifty yards away. The wreckage of Loveless's train was nowhere to be seen.

Loveless himself was in his wheelchair, sitting on the back deck of the *Wanderer*, shielded from the sun by a parasol and attended by two of his amazons.

"I don't think we're in Texas anymore," Gordon whispered.

West nodded minutely. "How long would that sleeping gas of yours knock us out for?"

"I'm not certain. With the strong dose we got, perhaps as much as a day."

West frowned. "A train can cover a lot of miles in a day."

This time it was Gordon's turn to nod almost imperceptibly, then to roll his eyes in Loveless's direction. "What do you suppose the little creep wants?"

"There's one way to find out." West took a deep breath, set his jaw, and started walking towards Loveless.

Gordon grabbed him just as he was about to step over the small fence. "Stop! Don't move!"

Loveless looked to Lippenreider. "Well?"

Lippenreider continued to peer through her opera glasses and speak in a flat monotone. "West: Get your hands off my thigh, you . . . Gordon: Listen to me. Loveless has collared us with the same magnetic device we found on Professor Morton."

Loveless turned to Munitia, who was engaged in loading two large metal disks into a complex mechanism with two spring-loaded throwing arms. "Munitia dear, I hope we're not going to leave evidence behind, as we apparently did last time."

Munitia shook her head. "No, sir. No boomerangs this time." She patted the disk she was holding very gently. "I used nitroglycerine instead." She finished setting up the device and flipped a switch. A prominent red light began to glow.

Loveless turned his head so that he was looking at West and Gordon again, and picked up a megaphone. "Good day, gentlemen! I trust you slept badly!"

Gordon's voice came back to Loveless as a distant shout. *"What have you done with Rita?"*

"Oh, it's Rita now, is it? How touchingly familiar! *Rita* is sleeping off the aftereffects of the gas in my stateroom!" Loveless looked toward the closed bedroom door. "Quite lovely, isn't she? Who knows, I may even become 'touchingly familiar' with her myself!"

This time it was Gordon who took the furious step toward Loveless and West who stopped him.

"You lay one grubby finger on her," West shouted, *"and that will be just one more reason why I track you down and kill you, you sawed-off little gelding!"*

For a moment Loveless flushed so furiously that his megaphone quivered—then he caught himself, and forced a smile. "Yes, Captain West, I'm sure that a well-endowed blackamoor such as yourself must find it absolutely incomprehensible that a white woman might enjoy carnal pleasure with a 'freak' such as myself. But having witnessed my usage of mechinology thus far, don't you think it would be child's play for me to create a machine that replicates the lower half of a male body, provides the requisite pumping action, and is both remarkably well equipped and indefatigably *steely?*"

Munitia and Lippenreider both shared a secret smile at that, apparently inspired by some mutual memory. West suddenly found himself quite unsettled by their smiles.

"And speaking of hard pumping," Loveless added,

"full steam ahead, Mister Coleman!" Coleman popped his head out the window of the locomotive and gave West and Gordon a terribly sad look. Amazonia popped out the window next to him and pressed a gun against the side of Coleman's head.

Coleman ducked back into the cab. With a blast of steam and the slow chuffing of pistons, the *Wanderer* slowly ground into forward motion.

"What a marvelous train!" Loveless crowed. "You don't mind if I borrow it, do you? Other than a lack of wheelchair access, I've found it a most comfortable way to pass the long miles from Texas to my laboratory in Spider Canyon! In fact, I believe I may ride it all the way to Promontory Point! You see, your president and I have a rendezvous with destiny!"

"*I'm sure he's looking forward to it!*" Gordon shouted. "*We warned him! He's got more than a thousand troops with artillery waiting for you, and your land ironclad is nothing but scrap!*"

"I guess I'll just have to manage!" Loveless retorted, as he faded into the distance, laughing like a madman.

West watched the train until it disappeared around the bend, then looked at Gordon. "I thought you said you couldn't get the telegraph working."

Gordon shook his head. "I couldn't. But Loveless doesn't know that."

"So what kind of troops does Grant actually have with him?"

"The 4th Nebraska."

West's eyes went wide. "Gordon, that's a *marching band!*"

"They're army, aren't they?"

"Hardly." West turned away from Gordon and looked in the direction the train had gone. A plume of smoke and steam rose in the distance. The chugging of the pistons echoed faintly from the hills. "You think he's really left us here?" West asked.

"I'd say so."

West took a deep breath, let it out, and turned to Gordon again. "Okay. Break out your little tool kit and let's get these damned collars off." West tugged at the irritating thing. Gordon unbuttoned his linen shirt, dipped a hand inside, and withdrew a flat leather case. Popping the snap with his thumb, he shook the case open.

It was empty, save for a small, folded, square of paper. Gordon unfolded the paper and read it out loud. *"Welcome to the Loveless Experimental Reeducation Camp for Political Dissidents! There are no guards! There is no barbed wire! There is nothing to hold you here except for your own desire to stay alive! As long as you remain within the designated perimeter, you will be perfectly safe!"*

West peeked over Gordon's shoulder at the note, then considered the knee-high wire fence. "And if we step outside the perimeter?"

Gordon turned the note over. The other side was blank. "It doesn't say."

"Well, then how do we know it isn't just a load of bull?

Maybe this is another one of Loveless's sick little mind games. Maybe *nothing* happens if we step over the wire."

Gordon shrugged. "Personally, I tend to believe Professor Morton. But go ahead; try it. Step over the fence and find out. Rita and I will put flowers on your grave every year."

West looked at Gordon. He reconsidered the fence. He looked at the tiny trail of far-off smoke that marked the rapidly receding train, and squinted up at the sun, high in the robin's-egg blue sky.

"I ain't got time for this," West growled.

"Wait!" Gordon exclaimed. He dropped to one knee and hiked his other pants cuff up. "I just remembered, I have an auxiliary tool kit!" He peeled back the top of his boot to reveal a row of shining tools and looked up, grinning expectantly.

West was standing on the other side of the fence. "See?" West said. "Nothing happened. I'm out." He hopped over the fence to land beside Gordon. "I'm in." He jumped across the boundary again, then started to skip back and forth. "Out, in. In, out." He stopped moving. "See? It was a load of bull." Gordon didn't answer. Instead, he listened intently as a low, droning buzz filled the air.

West cocked his head. "What the hell is *that?* A cicada? The mother of all hummingbirds?" Out of the corner of his eye, West caught a flash of sunlight off something small, metallic, and fast-moving. It appeared to be skimming along just above the tops of the grain and curving toward him.

Gordon leaped over the wire, hit West in the small of the back, and took him facedown into the dirt, a hair-thin fraction of a second before the gleaming silver buzz-saw blade slashed through the space where West's throat had been.

West flipped over, bounced to his feet, and jumped back over the fence. "*I'm in!*"

"*Too late!*" Gordon pointed to a second silver blur climbing high in the sky, to join the first one as it banked around for another pass. "*Run!*" he shouted, as if West needed instructions. West took off like he had wheels.

Gordon passed him a few yards later. *Damn, for a guy who eats that much, he sure can move!* West thought. He found breath enough for a quip. "Is it . . . too late . . . to take . . . these collars off?"

Gordon didn't look back. "Listen to the sound! When it changes pitch, it's going to dive!" West shut up and focused on the low, droning buzz. Abruptly, it shot up an octave and doubled in loudness. West hit the dirt.

Shredded green stalks and stems showered him as the disk narrowly missed his head and cut a long swath through the grain instead. West suddenly felt a breath of cool air on the back of his head and slapped a hand on it. The disk had damn near scalped him. He looked up.

Gordon was standing, and scanning the sky. "I can't see . . ." His hand shot out and pointed. "*There!*" He took off running in a new direction. West popped to his feet and followed him.

"Nice haircut," Gordon panted, as West caught up with him. "Very stylish. Now *dodge!*" Gordon dived left, West dived right, and the twin flying buzz saws screamed between them.

"Zigzag!" Gordon shouted hoarsely, as he got to his feet again, albeit a bit more slowly this time. "Maybe they can't . . . lock on target . . . if we keep changing direction." Gordon lurched off. West followed, scrambling in more or less the same direction. They cut through the field. They twisted, and dodged. Gordon abruptly stopped to wheeze. *Good sprinter but no endurance*, West noted. *Bet he can't jump, either.* The droning shifted in pitch.

"Down!" barked West, as he tackled Gordon. The twin blades slashed through the air mere inches behind West's butt. Leaves and flower tops flew like lawn clippings.

"Got an idea!" West said, as he dragged Gordon to his feet and got him moving again. "There's a gully . . . over yonder!"

"Can't keep running," Gordon complained. He zigged left.

"You got to!" West zagged right.

"Can't breathe!" Gordon staggered right.

"Won't *need* to breathe . . . without a head!" West cut left.

"Gotta rest!" Gordon stumbled left.

"No! Make for that gully!" West darted right, burst out of the grainfield—and stopped, dead in his tracks, waving his hands for balance. It wasn't a gully.

It was the edge of a hundred-foot cliff. A thin ribbon of muddy brown water snaked through the canyon far below.

A moment later Gordon lurched out of the grainfield, to end up on the edge of a small finger point just twenty feet away from West—assuming West could fly.

"Uh-oh," Gordon said.

"Here's the plan!" West shouted. "When I give the word, you jump off the cliff into my arms!"

All exhaustion instantly vanished from Gordon's face. *"WHAT? ARE YOU OUT OF YOUR MIND?"*

West pointed up. "They're coming 'round again." The droning hum Doppler-shifted as the disks banked in a long, graceful curve. For a moment the flying disks were almost beautiful, as they gleamed brilliantly in the sunlight. "On five! One! Two!"

Gordon shook his head. "Forget it! I won't do it!"

The hum shot up an octave and doubled in volume.

"FIVE!" West bellowed. He jumped, and involuntarily, so did Gordon. They collided in midair—as did the disks, about ten feet above their heads. The blast was deafening, but for West and Gordon, mostly harmless.

Artemus Gordon was without question a man of science. Even as he plummeted toward the river below he was able to deduce that—factoring in the Earth's gravitational constant of 32 feet/second^2—he had but three seconds to come to grips with his new dilemma:

"I CAN'T SWIM!"

"DON'T WORRY! THE FALL WILL PROBABLY KILL YOU!"

Inside the *Wanderer*, a wireless telegraph chattered out a short message. Munitia dutifully transcribed the code on her steno pad, then brought it over to Loveless, who was sitting in the galley, sorting through the wine rack. "Both disks have detonated," Munitia said.

Loveless digested this news a moment, then broke into a broad and toothy grin. "Well glory hallelujah. I do believe this turn of events warrants a celebration." He snatched a bottle of LaFitte '51 off the rack, tore off the foil seal, twisted away the wire, and fired the cork across the cabin. It pinged off the wall, shattered a lamp chimney, and forced Munitia to duck as it ricocheted past.

Lippenreider found a set of champagne flutes and held them, while Loveless, with considerable slop and spillage, poured. He raised his glass in a toast.

"Today, James West; tomorrow, Ulysses Grant! *To the final victory, my loves!*"

After the toast, Amazonia picked up the champagne cork and considered it. "Why does it do that?" she asked.

Loveless blinked uncertainly. "Why does what do what?"

"The champagne cork. Why does it shoot out of the bottle like that?"

"Well," Loveless said slowly, as he framed his answer, "the interior of the champagne bottle is under considerable carbon dioxide gas pressure. When you take off the wire and crack the seal on the cork, the base of the cork becomes the weak point in the container wall, and the shape of the bottle serves to focus the gas pressure on this small area, with the result that the cork is expelled at high velocity."

Amazonia dropped the cork and scooped up a handful of spent .45-70 shells from West's Gatling. "Why don't we do this with cartridges?" she asked. "Shape them like little champagne bottles, so that the gas pressure from the burning gunpowder is focused on the base of a small, high-velocity bullet? This would give us a flatter trajectory, greater range, and more striking power. You could call it a—oh, what's that word for a full-sized champagne bottle?"

"A magnum," Munitia suggested helpfully.

"Yes," Amazonia said, nodding. "Call it a *magnum*."

Loveless just shook his head. "Of all the silly . . . Amazonia my dear, please stick to what you're good at, breaking things and hurting people. I will be the genius here, if you don't mind."

Like a tired, aching, and filthy alligator, West crawled up onto the riverbank and flopped belly down to rest. Gordon, also soaking wet and covered head to toe in sticky, smelly, river-bottom muck, flopped down beside him and rolled over on his back.

"Pretty good plan, huh?" West asked, between gasps for breath.

Gordon merely glared at him.

CHAPTER ELEVEN

West and Gordon trudged on across the desolate and seemingly endless sagebrush flat. Cruel blue mirages danced and rippled like pools in the distance. High overhead the blazing sun beat down without mercy, eclipsed by the occasional circling buzzard.

"Water," Gordon moaned. "Water, please. A tall glass of seltzer over cracked ice with a twist of lime, *s'il vous plaît.*"

"Shut up," West suggested.

"And after that, *garçon*, I would like a nice thick filet mignon, medium rare, not overdone, smothered with sautéed mushrooms and onions. No, not the Bordeaux; I think a dry Burgundy might be more appropriate."

"Shut up," West advised.

Gordon stopped walking and defiantly put his hands

on his hips. "Why? If I'm going to die out here, I may as well die daydreaming about things that make me happy."

"We're not gonna die, unless you do something stupid. Dragging that magnetic collar along is stupid. Wastes strength. Talking is stupid. Wastes moisture. Ditch that magnet, keep your mouth shut, and breathe through your nose." West resumed trudging.

Gordon considered the magnetic collar he was holding. "James, while I realize that a magneto of this power may not inspire your scientific curiosity, it does mine. Besides, you never know when it might come in handy." Gordon looked up, realized West was leaving him behind, and scampered after him. "And I still don't see why we couldn't go back to the railroad track and wait for help."

"Think it through," West said. "If you were Loveless, what would be the most important thing on your mind?"

"Learning to tap-dance?"

West scowled at the feeble joke. "No, getting to Utah, to kill Grant. Would you waste a day waiting for two Federal agents to wake up, just so's you could insult 'em before killing 'em?"

Gordon nodded thoughtfully. "When you put it that way, probably not."

"So he obviously repaired the track, abandoned the ironclad, and took us along for the ride 'til we woke up. Killing us was just a sideshow. Not even worth sticking 'round for the finale."

Gordon arched an eyebrow. "He repaired the track? How?"

"Amazonia and Coleman did it, most likely. The rails were laid by hand. They can be taken up and moved by hand. If you're only worried about where you're *going*, the handiest source of spare parts is to rip up the track *behind* you." West abruptly realized he was doing exactly what he'd told Gordon not to do, and shut up. Silently, he marched on.

Gordon caught up with him again and tugged at his sleeve. "But I still don't understand why—"

"*Think,* Gordon. In two, maybe three days, another train comes along and finds the track all tore up. Loveless's engine ruined a hundred yards of roadbed when it blew. So figure it takes the Union Pacific another week to get a derrick out there to hoist the wreck off the tracks, and another week after that to fix the roadbed and lay new track. Three weeks later, a train finally comes through and picks us up. What do we do then?"

Gordon gulped. "Try to explain how we screwed up to Vice President Schuyler Colfax?"

"*President* Schuyler Colfax," West corrected.

Gordon stopped a moment to shudder at that thought, then set his jaw in a grim scowl and strode after West. His fierce resolve lasted almost two minutes.

"All the same," Gordon muttered, "I would sell my soul for a drink of water." West stopped abruptly, glared at Gordon, then popped the blade out of the toe of his boot. For a moment Gordon panicked, thinking he'd finally pushed West over the edge.

West's right foot lashed out—and kicked a neat hole in the side of a barrel cactus. "There's your water," West said, as a thin, clear stream dribbled out of the hole. Gordon dived beside the cactus, greedily splashing the water on his face, trying to figure out how to drink without impaling himself on the cactus spines. From this angle Gordon noticed a small burrow in the side of another cactus, and a pair of large eyes blinking at him. The eyes belonged to a bird; an owl of some kind.

Gordon made a grab for the owl. "I've found our lunch!"

"*No!*" West jumped between Gordon and the cactus and almost stomped his hands. "Don't touch the owl! The owl is *sacred!*"

Gordon recoiled and sat up.

West checked the bird to make sure it was okay, then turned to look at Gordon and shake his head.

"Man, for a Harvard grad, you sure don't know *nothin'*."

Night fell like a heavy blue cloak, accompanied by a chill and piercing wind. West led Gordon into a stand of rimrock and dumped the pieces of cholla wood he'd been collecting all during the day. "We camp here," West said.

Gordon shivered, and for a moment felt deeply grateful that West had stopped him from taking off and throwing away his shirt. "Why here? Why not push on?"

"Too dangerous. The predators come out at night."

Gordon looked at the dark and desolate wilderness all around and snorted. "Predators? Jim, we have seen exactly one lizard, one owl, and two spiders all day! There is not enough life here to—"

"Life's here," West insisted. He knelt down and started breaking up sticks to form a tinder pile. "The desert's *thick* with it. Brush wolves, jackrabbits, rattlesnakes, Gila monsters; just that most of 'em are smart enough to sleep in the daytime, and only come out at night." Satisfied with his tinder pile, West took off his boot, popped out the knife blade, and used it to strike a few sparks off a rock. The tinder caught, and West crouched down to blow gently on the embers and bring the flames to life.

Gordon dropped the magnet and plunked wearily on the sand next to West. "That looks like a good idea." He took off his boots and shook out a goodly accumulation of sand and rocks, then set the boots aside and began to massage his aching feet.

"Don't do that," West said.

Gordon looked up. "Do what?"

"Leave your boots sit like that. Scorpions like to crawl inside 'em." West picked up his own boot, retracted the blade, gave it a thorough shaking out, then pulled it back on his foot. Gordon followed suit.

Gordon scratched his head, stared at West, and finally worked up the nerve to ask. "How come you know so much? I mean, about this desert."

West threw another small chunk of wood on the fire. "I used to live here."

"You mean, the army stationed you here?"

"No, before that. It's a long story."

Gordon gestured for West to go on. "I've got time."

"I don't." West stood and selected one of the thicker

sticks from pile of firewood. "The predators come out at night." He turned, and flashed Gordon a feral grin.

"And I'm a predator." West slipped away, into the darkness. Gordon was still shuddering when West spoke again, his voice coming from somewhere in the night. "Oh, and Artemus?"

"Yes, Jim?"

"Rattlesnakes like heat. If one should decide to snuggle up to you, don't jump, or scream, or do anythin' stupid like that, okay? Just give it a few minutes to get comfy, then grab it right behind the head and wring its neck. Rattlesnake tastes just like chicken, only with lots more ribs."

Gordon gulped. "Thanks for the advice, Jim." He scooted over and threw another stick on the fire. *Fat chance I'm going to sleep tonight!* In the distance, a coyote howled, sending cold shivers down Gordon's spine.

But despite that, Gordon was snoring when West returned with the evening's entrée.

The next day's march took them off the flats and into rocky country. Gordon noticed that the going seemed easier, but also slower. He also noticed that the magnet seemed to be five pounds heavier, he'd had to take his belt in two notches to keep his pants up, and his stomach had begun to growl like an entire pack of rabid wolves.

Gordon then noticed that he was lagging behind West again and caught up. "I feel like a roasting duck," Gordon complained, for about the hundredth time. "Baste me, please. Why can't I take my shirt off?"

" 'Cause you'll sunburn to death," West answered.

"Don't you people ever get sunburned?"

"I do," West snapped. "I just don't turn red as a lobster, like some pasty-faced crackers I know."

Gordon ignored the verbal jab. "*Lobster*," he said with an ecstatic sigh. "Maine lobster, broiled. Clarified butter. Mashed potatoes, heaped up like a mountain, with little waterfalls of Bernaise sauce."

"Shut up," West said.

"Lobster thermidor. Lobster Newberg. Lobster *al fresco*."

"Bugs," West said.

Gordon wrinkled his nose. "Huh?"

"Your lobsters. They're just great big water bugs. Would you like to eat a handful of ants and locusts?"

Gordon's stomach somersaulted. "*Please!*"

"The People do," West said. "Some years, about the only crop that grows out here is locusts. So you catch a big mess of 'em, and roast 'em over a low fire . . ."

Gordon felt his gorge rising. "For God's sake, West!"

"And drip wild honey on 'em if you've got it; otherwise, you mix in a handful of live sugar ants. . . ."

Gordon tasted bile in the back of throat. "Jim, stop!"

West smacked his lips. "Mm-mmm! Sweet and crunchy!"

The world was spinning madly. Gordon stopped walking, seized an idea, and used it in a desperate attempt to hold his digestive system steady. "You said, 'The People.' *What* people?"

West turned around, looked at Gordon, and spread his

hands. "The people who live here. The Dineh. The Lords of the Earth." Gordon arched an eyebrow.

"The Spanish named 'em Navajo," West translated.

Gordon felt his stomach stabilize, and looked around nervously. "We're in Navajo territory?"

West nodded. "I think so." As an afterthought, he added, "I sure hope so."

Gordon sagged, and plunked down on a convenient rock outcropping. "You *hope* so?"

West came over and sat down next to him. "It's like this. We were in Texas. We were on our way to Utah. That means there's only about a half dozen places where Loveless could have dumped us." West craned his neck, and looked around. "This don't look like Cherokee country."

"Is that good?"

West shrugged. "Maybe. A lot of Cherokees fought for the South. They had some kind of side deal with Jefferson Davis."

Gordon nodded. "I see. So where are we exactly?"

West stroked his chin. "Not Arapaho or Cheyenne territory, that's for sure. They'd have killed us already." Gordon's eyes widened in alarm. "The Colorado militia tried to wipe out the Arapaho about five years back," West explained. "Chief Black Kettle ain't the forgiving type."

Gordon nodded again. "Very good. Then where—"

"We're too far north to be in Apache territory," West went on, "too far from the mountains for the Utes, and the ground is way too dry for the Pueblos."

Gordon slapped an open palm on his leg. "Dammit,

Jim, I'm a marshal, not an anthropologist! Where in the blazes are we?"

West took off his cowboy hat, scratched his head a bit, and fiddled with his hatband some. "I don't rightly know," he admitted at last. "But I do know this: Gordon, when you were in Washington, did you ever happen to meet Kit Carson?"

Gordon nodded and smiled. "Why, yes I did. *Marvelous* man. Intelligent, charming, *très* debonair—"

"Yeah, well, out here, a lot of people feel kind of differently about him. If we do happen to meet up with any Navajo, I wouldn't go throwing his name around, if I were you."

Gordon crouched by the crackling fire, listening to the evening serenade of the coyotes and munching on a roasted reptile leg. "Hmm," he said, between bites and chews. "This Gila monster . . . it needs something."

"It needs you to pass it over here, is what it needs," West grumbled. Gordon tore another leg off the blackened carcass and handed it to West, who bit into it with caveman relish.

Gordon shook his head and ignored the appalling growling, slurping, crunching, and utter lack of table manners on West's part. "No, I'm thinking . . . a touch of paprika. And maybe cilantro. With a nice little diced green pepper salad on the side, some tomatillos, and . . . rice, that's it! A brown rice casserole in a black-bean sauce! Why, there's a whole new *world* of cuisine out

here, just waiting to be discovered! I think I'll call it . . .
Aboriginal Nueva Hispaniola del, uh . . ."

"*Southwestern food* is too simple, huh?"

Gordon scowled. "Shut up and eat your lizard."

West gladly did so.

A minute or two later, Gordon ruined it by talking
again. "Sorry for that last remark, Jim."

West, who'd already forgotten it, looked up. "Huh?"

"It's just that . . . I'm not quite myself, out in this . . .
awful wilderness." Gordon glanced around nervously at
the dark night, and the strange long shadows cast by the
campfire. He cleared his throat and recited from memory:

> " 'A thousand fantasies throng the mind,
> of calling shapes, and beckoning shadows dire,
> on sands and shores and desert wilderness.'

"—John Milton," Gordon finished.

West finished gnawing the last bit of good meat off a
Gila monster femur, threw the bone into the fire, and
wiped his mouth on the back of his hand. "You know,
Gordon," he said, "the most amazing guy I ever knew
was this Navajo shaman. He could make gunshot wounds
heal overnight and—"

"Yes, do tell," Gordon interrupted. "I am dying to
know how you have come to know so much about the
ways of these savages."

West shot Gordon a narrow, dirty look. "First off, Gordon, they ain't savages. Down in Arizona the *anasazi*—
the Old Ones—have brick cities that are more than a

thousand years old. You *belaga'ana* got anything like that?"

Taken aback by West's anger, Gordon stroked his chin. "Well, Rome, of course, and then there's Constantinople—but that word you used. Bela . . . ?"

"*Belaga'ana*," West repeated. "It means, uh, white guys." *Well no, that's not exactly what it means, but that's about as close a translation as Gordon can probably handle.*

"Bel . . ." Gordon rolled it around his tongue once or twice, then gave up trying to pronounce it. "You speak Navajo, then? Did you learn it while you were stationed out here?"

West shook his head. "I was never stationed out here."

Gordon was puzzled. "But I thought you had considerable military experience vis-à-vis the red man?"

"If visawhatsis means 'against,' yeah, I do. But that was mostly up in Minnesota and Dakota territory, against the Sioux." West stopped talking, and stared into the fire. Whatever memory the subject had called up, it was inaccessible to Gordon, and West didn't seem in the mood to share.

After half a minute of silence, broken only by the soft crackling of the fire, Gordon sensed the need to prompt West. "Please," he said. "Go on."

West picked up a stick, used it to stir the fire a bit, then dropped the stick into the flames. He watched the stick catch fire, then looked up at Gordon with an unreadable expression.

"Well, Artemus, while all you *belaga'ana* geniuses out

East were busy trying to figure out the best way to destroy the country, the native folks out West were keeping a sharp eye on your forts and troop movements. By '63 they'd figured out that something really big was happening on the other side of their world, and that they were never going to have a better shot at kicking you out of *their* country. Between '63 and '65, the U.S. Army fought nearly ninety battles with the Sioux, the Nez Percé, the Apaches, the Cheyenne—and yeah, with the Navajo. There were massacres and atrocities enough to go around for both sides, and I'll tell you one thing for sure: If the Indians had been able to *coordinate* a little better, and if Chief Joseph had had modern rifles, the United States today would end at the east bank of the Mississippi River!"

Gordon blinked. "I had no idea."

West realized he'd gotten agitated, took a deep breath, and settled down. "Of course you don't. It rarely made the East Coast papers. You folks had far bigger fish to fry, and Lincoln couldn't spare front-line troops to make the frontier safe. So instead, he sent us. The 9th Negro Cavalry."

West took another deep breath and sat up a little straighter, as if he was in a saddle.

"You know what the Sioux called us? *Buffalo soldiers*. You see, they'd never seen a black man before, so they didn't know what to make of us. We dressed like the red-leg U.S. soldiers they'd come to hate, and we acted kind of like white men, but we were big, and dark, and strong, and we had all this curly black hair on top of our heads, just like—"

"Like buffalo," Gordon completed.

West shrugged. "They seemed to think we were some kind of crossbreed."

Gordon envisioned the biological concept for a moment, then sputtered. "Buffalo soldiers!"

"Yeah, well, go ahead and laugh. It got a little old after a while, having Indian prisoners ask if it was your momma or your daddy who was the buffalo." West sighed.

Gordon let out one last chuckle, then fell serious. "Well, I expect General Custer won't have that problem."

"Nope," West agreed. "Now that the 7th Cavalry is out there, the Sioux will have no choice but to settle down." The two men nodded a while, in silent agreement. West reached over and tore off a chunk of Gila monster's tail.

"So," Gordon said presently. "This still doesn't answer my original question. How did you learn to speak Navajo? Your parents were, what, settlers out here?"

West almost choked on his lizard. He coughed, cleared his throat, then resumed chewing.

"My parents were slaves," West said softly.

Gordon blanched. "Omigod. I'm sorry. I—"

"The—master—had a bad year. Weevils in the cotton. Needed to raise cash fast. He sold me down the river when I was eight years old." West suddenly lost interest in the meat and spit it out.

Gordon tried again. "I—"

There was no point trying to interrupt; West's narration was clearly on autopilot. "I ran away as soon as my legs were long enough to take me. Couldn't go back to my family; even if they hadn't been sold themselves, I'd just get whipped, or maybe hanged. Couldn't go north; the way was too well watched, and besides, the Fugitive Slave Act was law. Even if I made it to a Free State, I wouldn't be safe.

"So I went west. And lucked out. Fell in with a band of Navajo, and they adopted me." West spread his arms in an expansive gesture, to take in the night, the desert, and everything. "This here is the only real home I've ever known." He raised his arms and looked at the sky. "I lived ten years out here, on Mother Earth, under Father Sky. Then one day a troop from the 10th Negro Cavalry rode through, and said there was a big war on, out East. Said it was a war to end slavery. The next morning I kissed my adopted parents good-bye, hiked down to Fort Defiance, and enlisted in the U.S. Army."

Gordon had one question burning in his mind, but another that decency required him to ask first. "Jim, after the war: your real parents, your real family. Did you ever . . . ?"

"I found 'em," West said softly.

"And then I buried 'em, in the churchyard at New Liberty."

CHAPTER TWELVE

Jim West lay on his back on the cool desert sand, hands clasped behind his head, staring up at the night sky. The stars sparkled overhead like a fortune in diamonds and sapphires spread out on a lush blanket of inky black velvet, and the sky slowly turned, like a great, glittering, crystalline wheel.

West's mind wandered as he lay, from soft and wistful memories of things done and faces gone a long time ago, to sharp-edged plans for things to be done and people desperately in need of a proper killing in the next day or two, to the strange, lucid dreams that still haunted him all these years after his vision quest, and his journey with Badger through the Fourth World.

Most of all, though, West lay awake, earnestly wishing with all his heart and soul that Artemus Gordon would shut up.

A soft commotion broke out in the greasewood, about fifty yards off. There was a sudden hissing, a rattle of leaves, a piteous squeal, and a violent thrashing —

And just as suddenly, a terrible silence.

"*What was that?*" Gordon whispered urgently.

"Rattlesnake killin' a rat," West answered, wearily.

"I thought they always rattled before they struck."

"The rattle's a warning. It means, 'Go away, I'm armed.' Snakes don't warn critters they're plannin' to eat." West rolled his head slightly to the side and tried to spot Gordon in the dark. "Don't worry, Arte. Rattlesnakes almost never try to eat people." One large and lumpy shadow on the other side of the burned-out campfire shifted uncomfortably.

West allowed himself a thin smile and went back to watching the stars. A meteor flashed across the heavens, traveling west to east. A cricket whose biological imperative to mate had overcome his instinct for self-preservation began advertising his presence by chirping nearby. In the distance, one lonely coyote howled and waited for an answer that never came.

"I'm cold," Gordon complained.

"You said that before," West pointed out.

"Yeah, well I'm still cold. The desert gets so blasted hot during the day, you'd think it'd be a little warmer at night."

"You would think that," West said. "But this time of year, we're just lucky it's not snowing."

"*Snow?*" Gordon sucked in his breath, and his teeth

started chattering. Strangely, West derived no satisfaction from making Gordon squirm this time.

"Fire," Gordon said. "Fire is good. Fire is our friend."

West rolled his head to the side again and saw Gordon trying to creep closer to the dead ashes in the fire pit. "Gordon?" he asked. "Why do harbors have light-houses?"

Gordon thought it over. "To guide incoming ships?"

"Exactly. You want everyone within five miles to know where we are, you go ahead and light that fire. Me, I think I'll go sleep somewhere else if you do that."

Gordon considered West's words, backed away from the fire pit, and tried to curl up like a dog. After shivering for a while and trying a series of positions that varied only in their degrees of discomfort, he hesitantly said, "You know, uh, we could, er—share body heat."

West sat up and tried to figure out where Gordon's head was, so he could glare the man straight in the eye. "*No. Way. In. Hell.*" Gordon didn't answer.

West flopped back down on the sand and bristled a bit.

The stars turned in their slow and eternal courses.

In the distance, the coyote howled again.

"Jim?" Gordon asked. "How much longer 'til day-break?"

West looked at the stars. "About six hours."

"Are you sure?"

"Yeah."

"How? I mean, is this your Navajo magic again?"

"Nope." West raised an arm and pointed at the sky. "The sky is a big clock, Gordon. Moon set around the time the Archer rose. Now the Old Man with a Stick is setting in the northwest. This time of year, that means it's about half past midnight, and dawn is in six hours."

Gordon snorted. "*Astrology.*"

"Nope. *Astronomy.* You white guys don't have a monopoly on science, you know. The Navajo shamans have been watching these skies for over a thousand years."

Gordon shook his head. "Like I said," he insisted. "Magic, superstition, and astrology."

West thought it over. "Maybe shaman isn't the right word. Maybe you'd have more respect if I said *rabbi.* The shaman is a teacher; he knows the religious laws, the prayers, the medicine, and the history of the People since the beginning of time. What does that sound like to you?"

Gordon paused a long time before answering.

"A rabbi," he said at last. "Point conceded."

West went back to watching the stars. The coyote in the distance yipped a few times, then let out an unbelievably long and mournful howl. West smiled.

The trickster god, Coyote, was his friend.

A horrible, weird, rasping noise woke West with a start. His eyes snapped open. He grabbed for the gun that wasn't there. He got a flash take on his situation—

It was about three in the morning, and Gordon was snoring like a ripsaw. West stretched out across the sand and gave Gordon a hard nudge in the shoulder. "Hey. Stop that."

Gordon snorked and sat up. "Huh? Wha—?"

"You're snoring, man. Stop it."

Gordon shook his head groggily. "I do not snore."

"Do too. Now cut it out." West crawled back to his slightly warm spot in the sand and stretched out again. "Some people 'round here got to sleep," he muttered, as he drifted off. His breathing became a soft, rhythmic, susurration.

Gordon, now fully awake, flopped down on the sand—wiggled, squirmed, picked out a sharp rock and tossed it aside—then tried to find sleep again. He was just starting to doze off when a horrible thought crossed his mind and made his eyes pop wide open again.

"*Jim?*" he whispered urgently.

"Mmm?" West responded, after a fashion.

"Do you think Rita is all right?"

"Rita who?" West mumbled. He rolled away from Gordon.

Gordon crawled over beside West and shook him awake. "Rita Escobar! The professor's daughter! Do you think Loveless—?" Gordon shuddered at the thought.

West glared at Gordon over his shoulder. "Artemus, what makes you so sure she ain't been working for Loveless all along? I mean, the way she 'accidentally' touched off that sleeping gas grenade, just when I had Loveless disarmed and in a can . . ." West left the thought hanging.

Gordon grew indignant. "Jim, if you'd seen her in that cage in Loveless's bedroom—"

"I've seen a *lot* of weird things in bedrooms," West said. "A cage would be pretty tame for some women I know. And if you'd seen Miss East, like I did . . ." West wisely decided to shut his mouth at that point, and sat up.

Gordon was aghast. "Surely you aren't suggesting—"

"I am. Maybe Rita was planted in that room, just in case someone like you busted in. I mean, Loveless has got something way strange goin' on with the women. It's like a cult or something: Amazonia, Munitia, and Lippenreider—and Miss East—would do *anything* for that sawed-off little freak. Who's to say Miss Rita isn't one of 'em?"

Gordon planted his hands on his hips. "I am. And I will ask you, sir, to take back the aspersion you have cast upon the lady's honor!"

West lay down and rolled on his side, putting his back to Gordon again. "I'll do no such thing, Arte. If she's still alive, the lady can defend her honor herself. And I'll ask you to start thinking with your brains 'stead of your *co-jones*."

Flummoxed, Gordon crawled back over to his side of the fire pit, and tried to go to sleep.

In the distance, Coyote laughed and sang.

"Jim?" Gordon asked softly, wondering if West was asleep.

"What?" West answered, obviously awake and annoyed.

"I just wanted to say, I'm really sorry."

"Fine. Now shut up let me get to sleep."

Gordon held silent a minute or so, then sighed heavily and tried again. "No, I mean I'm sorry for you, and for your family."

West considered ignoring Gordon, but realized he was

never going to get any sleep until he let Gordon expel this latest clot of tangled thoughts. "What the Hell are you talking about?"

"I keep trying to imagine what it must have been like. I mean, to be a . . . slave."

"You can't," West snapped. "So don't even try."

Gordon sighed. "Jim," he said presently, "I *must* try. It's how I . . . get inside people's heads. How I understand them."

"I don't *want* you inside my head, Gordon. It's crowded enough in here already. You'd be bringin' in all them dresses and fancy cooking pots and such."

"Please, Jim."

West started to snap an answer, then caught himself and paused. *I'm so mad I'm shaking*, he realized with a bit of surprise. *Okay, let's try giving Gordon what he wants*. West rolled over to face Gordon and propped himself up on one elbow.

"You wanna know what it's like to be a slave?" he asked softly, trying to control the tremor in his voice. "Picture this: You are *nothing*. You don't own nothing, you can't ever be nothing, you are *livestock*, to be bought, sold, traded, or lost in a poker game. Your mother is a brood sow—if you're real lucky you know who your real daddy is, and he might even be allowed to live with you sometimes. But some masters breed people like *hogs*, and you are just another little piglet that he's raising up until you're big enough to send to market.

"You don't have a *family*; slave marriages aren't legal.

You don't have a *life*; the master can whip you to death anytime he feels like it. You don't have *medicine*; the Man cares more for his horses than he does for a sick black child. You don't even have a proper *name*!"

West suddenly realized he was shouting at Gordon and stopped, to take a deep breath and get his temper under control.

When it was obvious West was taking a breather, Gordon asked, "So James T. West . . . ?"

"Is the name I made up the day I enlisted. Even I don't know what the 'T' stands for. It just sounded good."

"But when you lived among the Navajo . . . ?"

"Yes, I have a Navajo name. No, I'm not going to tell you what it is. I am not about to spend the rest of my life listening to you mispronounce it."

Gordon nodded. "Okay, fair enough. So—"

"My real name," West said, hoping to put the conversation to rest, "is *James*. That's what my mother named me. The last name doesn't matter; it was just the name of the family that owned us. Kind of like a property mark, you see. Most slave names are like that." West rolled onto his back again, clasped his hands behind his head, crossed his legs tightly, and resumed staring furiously at the silent stars.

After a while, Gordon said, "I *am* sorry, James."

"You said that already."

"No, I mean, obviously, I've hit a raw nerve."

"So don't hit it again."

"I won't. Good night, James." West heard rustling in the darkness, then the soft and steady sound of Gordon's breathing. Somewhere in the night, an owl hooted. Overhead, the beautiful but useless stars turned, grinding inevitably and eternally toward the west. West guessed it was perhaps another two hours until dawn.

The quietude started to get on West's nerves.

"All the same," West said, "it is kind of funny."

Gordon roused, sort of. "Huh?"

"I mean, think about it," West went on. "The Southerners sent their sons off to a stupid and bloody war, but kept their valuable *slaves* safe at home. Wonder what they're gonna do when they finally realize that they've got a shortage of white men and a surplus of white women?" West chuckled softly. "Another two or three generations, I think, and no one will know there ever was a Southern white or a Southern black. We'll all be just slightly different shades of brown. Maybe then we'll be ready for the Sixth World." West sighed, relaxed, and smiled, for what felt like the first time in days.

The stars above shone like all the brilliant jewels in the Crown of Creation.

"Sixth World?" Gordon asked, when it was apparent that West was done talking.

West raised an arm and pointed straight up. "*That* is the Sixth World. It's perfect. And when we're finally good enough, we get to live up there."

Gordon was puzzled. "You mean Heaven?"

"No, I mean the Sixth World." West rolled over and got up on an elbow again.

"You *belaga'ana* got shortchanged. You only got

kicked out of the Garden of Eden. The People believe we were kicked out of four other worlds before we got to this one—the Fifth World. But the thing is, each time we got booted out of a world, we wound up trading up to a *better* one.

"Until we got here, where we're so close to perfection that we can see its bottom side. And someday, when the People prove themselves worthy, the Gods will open up the gate of stars to let us climb up and live there."

West shrugged. "That's probably why the Navajo didn't put up too much of a struggle when Kit Carson came along to kick them out of Arizona. Most likely some shaman said, 'Okay, People, we've been kicked out of worlds before. We know what to do. We're on our way to someplace better.'" West shrugged again. "Even shamans get it wrong, sometimes, I guess."

Gordon was struggling to understand. "You mean if, say, a Navajo woman were to one day weave a perfect blanket, she'd die and just shoot straight up to Heaven?"

West shook his head. "No, dying has nothing to do with it. When it happens, it will happen to *all* the People at the same time—and some of the better Pueblos and Hopis, too—and the Fifth World will be left to you *belaga'ana*."

Gordon considered this a while. "I see," he said at last, "the classic end-of-time redemption and afterlife myth, as is common to so many primitive cultures. I expect the accompanying ceremonies and superstitions—"

West interrupted. "*Superstitions?* Gordon, I tried to tell you before, I've seen a shaman heal a gunshot wound overnight! I've watched 'em make pebbles roll along the ground just by looking at 'em! I knew one shaman who could turn himself into a *bird*—one time he turned into a crow and flew all the way to Galena, just to watch the Lincoln-Douglas debates!"

Gordon snorted derisively. "Oh, really? And which candidate did he prefer?"

"He came back and told us it really didn't matter which white man won the election, because either way the red man was going to lose. But my *point*, Gordon, is this man could do all these incredible things, yet he never bragged *half* as much as you do about how smart he was! And you with your Harvard education and all."

There was a long pause before Gordon answered. "As a matter of fact, I never attended college."

"Huh? But you got a Harvard class ring."

"Amazing what you find in pawnshops these days, isn't it?"

West sat up and stared at Gordon, mouth agape in amused wonder. "Why, Artemus Gordon! You are nothing but a dirty old *con man*!"

"Am not," Gordon sniffed. He, too, sat up, and struck a pose. "I'm an *actor.* And since it usually gets me a certain modicum of credibility and respect, I have learned to *act* as if I have a Harvard education."

West snorted. "Yeah, right. And I bet when you're in New York, you *act* as if you own Manhattan Island." West's face cracked into a broad grin, and he settled into a comfortable cross-legged sitting position. "Come on, dish it up. What's the real story? Medicine show? Snake-oil salesman? Or was your daddy a traveling rainmaker? And what *is* your real name, anyway? I mean, 'Artemus Gordon,' well . . ." West chuckled.

"That's my real name," Gordon said, with wounded pride. "And I am an actor, as were my parents. I was born and raised in an itinerant theater company. I grew up on the road, traveling from one podunk town to another, and while I never had a formal education, I did read voraciously. By the time I was twelve I'd devoured the complete Cambridge Shakespeare, as well as Plutarch and Herodotus. By the time I was twenty—"

"Let me guess," West interrupted. "You got bored with it all and decided to *act* like a U.S. Marshal."

Gordon cleared his throat. "No," he said rather testily, "I was starting to gain serious recognition as an actor. My parents retired from the road and settled down in New York, and I got an offer to join a highly respected repertory theatre company in Washington, D.C. The troupe was based out of Ford's Theater. Does that name mean anything to you?"

West's smiled collapsed. "Oh, my God . . ."

"There was another young man in the company: John Wilkes Booth, twenty-six years old. His father, Junius, was a great tragedian, and his brother, Edwin, was widely considered to be the best Shakespearian actor in America. Both of them were stout Union loyalists, but John Wilkes was a *Copperhead*, through and through, for no other reason than it seemed to annoy his parents. John was always full of a lot of hot radical talk about the Southern cause, but frankly, we laughed it off, because—

"Well, because we were actors, and had no great concern about the war, and also because John Wilkes Booth was handsome, yes, and had a beautiful voice, but he was not terribly *talented*, nor was he particularly bright. We used to call him 'the Virginia Ham' behind his back. One day he heard someone say that, and he said, 'But I'm from *Maryland*.' " Gordon stopped for breath.

"Were you there, the night Lincoln—?"

"I was *onstage*," Gordon said. "I was *in Our American Cousin*. There was this line I had in the third act; the biggest laugh line in the whole show. I noticed that Booth was hanging around backstage and acting strange that night, but didn't think anything of it because he wasn't in the show, and he *always* acted strange when he wasn't the center of attention. He said one last thing to me, just before I went on for the third act: 'You will remember this performance forever.'

"Then I went out there, did my scene, hit my marks, and delivered the laugh line. Brought the house down!

"You can't see anything past the proscenium when you're onstage with the footlights in your eyes. All I knew was that one moment the audience was roaring with laughter—and then Booth came flying in from a box seat, shouting '*Sic semper tyrannis!*' I heard his ankle snap when he hit the floor, and I remember thinking, *John, you idiot, what the Hell are you doing, upstaging me by ad libbing* Julius Caesar? The whole audience was kind of shocked, too. I mean, they *recognized* Booth, and were rustling through their programs, trying to find the credit that said, 'Tonight the part of the Limping Madman is performed by John Wilkes Booth.'

"Then we heard someone shout, *'The president has been shot!'* and Mrs. Lincoln started to scream. And while I and the rest of the company were milling about in utter panic and confusion, John Wilkes Booth hobbled out the back door, climbed on a waiting horse, and escaped."

Gordon sighed heavily and looked at West, sitting there silently. "I could have stopped him, James. Booth had a group of followers; losers like himself. He tried to take me into his confidence, but I didn't want anything to do with him. I could have told someone what I knew about John Wilkes Booth, *before* the president ever entered that theater.

"I could have saved Abraham Lincoln's life."

After a time, West nodded gently. "And that's why you decided to become a U.S. Marshal."

"Exactly."

West took a deep breath and let it out again. "We'd best get some sleep. We've got a busy day ahead of us tomorrow." West unfolded his legs, clasped his hand behind his head, and stretched out on the sand. After a brief hesitation, Gordon followed suit.

"Arte?"

"Yes, James?"

"Booth was right. You *will* remember that performance forever."

"Indeed." Gordon paused. "Good night, James."

West rolled his head to look at Gordon, and caught the first faint streak of rose on the eastern rim of the sky.

"Good morning, Arte."

CHAPTER THIRTEEN

Artemus Gordon awoke to the feeling of searing sunlight full on his face. His eyelids snapped wide open—and immediately slammed shut again, to shield his delicate retinas from the glare until his pupils had a chance to adjust. "My God," he muttered. "The sun's already up. It must be—" He put a hand over his face and risked a squint at the brilliant orb through the cracks between his fingers. He learned nothing except that the sun was, as usual, painfully bright. "Jim will know," Gordon decided. He rolled over to wake West.

There was an enormous hairy spider the size of a man's open hand perched nonchalantly on top of West's belly, basking in the warm sunlight and gently flexing its front legs. Gordon gasped.

"G'morning, Arte," West said softly.

Gordon was stunned. "You're awake?"

"Have been for about half an hour."

"Are you—?"

"I'm fine. And a long as this tarantula here doesn't get too startled, I will remain so. Please don't startle her."

Gordon hefted the magnet, decided it was too clumsy to use a weapon, then looked around helplessly for a stick or something. "Is there anything I can do?"

"I'm thinking about it." West pursed his lips. "Nope."

"But—"

"Watch and learn, Gordon. I was hoping she'd decide to mosey on all by herself. But the situation here changed about five minutes ago, and now if she doesn't leave soon, she's gonna be in a world of hurt."

Gordon stared at the spider. "I don't understand."

"Don't look at the tarantula. Look *above* it. You see something flying?"

Gordon looked where West indicated, and quickly spotted a small black shape, flitting, darting, and hovering. "You mean that bee?"

"That's a desert wasp, Gordon. It's one of the world's all-time great hunters. Absolutely fearless, willing to take on creatures a hundred times its own size—uh-oh. Here goes."

The wasp dived on the tarantula and sank its stinger into the spider's abdomen. The tarantula twisted, writhed, and bucked like a bronco with a burr under the saddle. For an instant Gordon caught a very clear glimpse of the spider's formidable half-inch venomous fangs, as it reared back —

Then tumbled over backwards and rolled off West's

stomach, quivering spastically. West practically flew to his feet.

"*Holy—!*" West started hyperventilating as if he hadn't drawn a breath in half an hour, which under the circumstances was probably a pretty fair assessment. "*Did you see—?*" He patted himself down rapidly, checking for bites. "*I mean, that sucker had fangs like—like—and—*"

West got a grip, slowed his breathing to normal, and recovered his usual cool and laconic veneer. "Hey, Arte, check this out." He squatted by the quivering tarantula and poked at it with a stem of grass.

Gordon stood up, but was perfectly content to stay where he was. "Jim, are you nuts?"

"No, really, it's okay. Wasp stung it. It's paralyzed."

"It looks more like it's having convulsions."

"Whatever." West abruptly dropped the stem of grass, stood up, and stepped back. "Whoa. Let's give the lady room to work." Gordon tried to figure out what West was talking about, then noticed that the black wasp had landed on the spider and was busy darting about, feelers questing, abdomen twitching. "She might need to . . . "

With a heroic effort, the tarantula suddenly stretched four legs and tried to flip over. The wasp clung tight and jabbed its stinger into the spider's unprotected belly, then stung it twice more.

The spider relaxed and lay still.

"Is it dead?" Gordon asked.

"Nope. It's lunch. Watch."

The wasp, apparently, was satisfied that the tarantula

was now in the required state. It flitted across the spider's body one last time, then darted over to the spider's head, fastened its mandibles onto something, and started tugging.

Gordon whistled. "Look at that! It's dragging the spider!"

West grinned. "You ain't seen nothing yet. You see that hole?" Gordon watched in silent amazement as the wasp slowly and laboriously dragged the spider over to a small hole in the dirt, then somehow managed to stuff the body down the tube. "Spider's still alive, but it's paralyzed. Now the wasp is gonna lay her eggs on it. In a couple of days the grubs will hatch out, and they'll find they got all the fresh, live spider they can eat. It'll take 'em about a week to devour the spider, and it'll be alive right up to the very end. That's how the wasp provides for her family."

West shook his head in admiration, then stood up and rubbed his hands together. "Hey, I don't know about you, but that makes me kind of hungry! Let's go rustle up some breakfast!" Without waiting for an answer, West strode off.

Sighing and shaking his head, Gordon followed.

By late morning the broken rimrock and foothills had given way to a maze of deep and narrow slickrock canyons. West and Gordon strode along side by side now, barely speaking, covering the miles at a rapid pace. Words no longer seemed necessary; without really thinking about it, Gordon and West had at last reached an understanding.

When they rounded another twist in the canyon, it also became apparent that they'd reached another dead end.

Gordon spoke. "You sure you know where we're going?"

West took off his cowboy hat, scratched his head, and considered the rockslide that blocked the gorge. "Yeah. Well, I'm *pretty* sure."

Gordon scowled at West.

"These canyons are tricky," West said defensively. "And I haven't ridden through Spider Canyon in about ten years."

Gordon crossed his arms.

" 'Sides, everything looks all different when you're on horseback."

Gordon shook his head. "We're lost, aren't we?"

"No," West said, a touch too quickly. "I mean, this is definitely Utah, and we are definitely in the right part of the Promontory Mountains. I can tell you that we are really *close* to Spider Canyon. But—"

"But we're still lost," Gordon said. "You don't have the slightest idea which way to turn, do you?"

West looked down and scuffed the ground with the toe of his boot. "Well . . ."

"Fine," Gordon snapped. He picked a direction at random and started off. When he didn't come back in a minute or two, West decided he might need some looking after.

He found Gordon around the next bend, lying flat on

his back, one arm stretched out over his head, holding the magnet. Despite the fact that he was lying down and not moving, some unseen force was dragging Gordon across the sand.

"Neat trick," West observed. "How are you doing that?"

"I'm not," Gordon protested. "It's the magnet. It seems to have developed a mind of its—oops!" The magnet slipped out of Gordon's fingers and shot away, to bury itself in the sand some forty yards away with a loud metallic *clang!* "What the—?" Gordon got to his feet and slapped the dust off his pants, then followed West over to where the magnet had impacted. West was carefully digging through the sand with the toe of his boot. Another inch or so, and he found what the magnet had been so excited about; a set of railroad tracks, buried by the drifting sand. West squatted down and looked at the brand on the tie.

"Union Pacific," West said, standing again. "Arte, I hate to admit it, but when you're right, you're right. These tracks should lead us right there."

Gordon nodded. "Well, I think our partnership has just taken a great leap forward. You've finally admitted I was right about something. Now, how about admitting that you were lost?"

West set his jaw, turned his face to the northwest, and started walking.

"Don't push it," he said.

West dropped to a crouch as they approached the top of the ridge, then took off his hat. "Over here," he hissed at

Gordon. "Rocks'll break up your silhouette against the skyline." Gordon crouched and followed. The two men covered the last few yards of the climb on their bellies, crawling like lizards across the loose talus. When they reached the cusp, they paused for breath, then cautiously peered over the rim, into Spider Canyon.

West whistled, soft and low. "Ho, boy. What do you make of that, Arte?"

"Very nice," Gordon muttered. "The Rock of Gibraltar meets the Palace of Versailles. Very impressive."

West cocked his head. "Huh?"

"Never mind." Gordon went back to studying the structure in the box canyon below. It was spectacular, in a deranged kind of way. Soaring Victorian spires mixed with Gothic arches and neoclassical domes. Everything appeared to be made of glass and steel, except for a plain and incongruous old wooden silo off to one side. The scale of the buildings simply dwarfed the humans who moved in and out of them, making the people look like so many ants crawling around inside a crystal sugar bowl.

"I don't suppose your Indian friends might have built a casino," Gordon suggested.

"Not a chance," West said. "Indians, generally, like to keep things simple."

West and Gordon studied the complex a while longer.

"So what's your idea?" Gordon asked at last.

West rubbed his sunburned nose. "Well, ideally I'd have B Troop set up the mountain howitzers on that ledge over there, so we could get plunging fire on the buildings.

Then I'd have C and A Troops dismount and take cover in those rocks over there, to provide enfilading fire with their rifles, while I led D Troop in a feint around the left side and tried to draw 'em out."

Gordon blinked and looked around. "Jim, in case you haven't noticed, we do not presently have a cavalry company at our disposal."

"I noticed." West frowned. "What've you got left?"

Gordon took quick inventory. "One sleeping-gas button, three lockpicks, a hacksaw and a rat-tail file."

"Not much of an offensive arsenal."

"Nope."

West went back to studying the complex. Gordon decided he wasn't going to learn anything more by looking at the buildings, and switched to scanning the surrounding canyons and plateaus. On his second sweep, he spotted something. He did a double take, then nudged West. "Jim!"

"Shh!" West looked up. "What?"

"Over there, to the right."

West looked in the indicated direction. "What, that pointy kinda thing?"

"No, above it."

"Those red rocks?"

"No, above *them*. On the playa, and a little more to the right. Behind all that sagebrush."

West broke into a broad grin. "Hot damn! The *Wanderer*! Does she look okay to you?"

Gordon shook his head. "I can't tell from here. We've got to get closer." He started to stand.

"*Down!*" West grabbed Gordon by the shirtfront and pulled him back to the ground. "*Company's coming!*"

A moment later, Gordon heard it too: a shrill, piercing whine, erratic in pitch but growing steadily in volume, accompanied by the heavy, dull, thudding and crunching sound of a steelworks drop forge. His first thought was to scan the skies for more flying buzzsaw blades, then he placed the whine, and remembered where he'd heard it before. "Steam turbine," he whispered to West. "The Royal Navy is experimenting with them in ships. But how on Earth—"

"*Loveless!*" West pointed, then grabbed Gordon and dragged him to cover behind a large boulder. Like a pair of terrified mice, the two men edged around the boulder and peered out.

At first, Loveless seemed to be sitting in a wheelchair suspended in midair, and wearing a sort of white Napoleonic admiral's uniform so laden with gold brocade it properly belonged in an Italian operetta. As he rose higher in the air it became apparent that the chair was perched on a flying bridge of some sort, and that Amazonia, Munitia, and Lippenreider were personing the complex banks of levers and controls arrayed before Loveless's seat. Next a pair of belching smokestacks hove into view, followed by a large cupola or dome, a complexity of interlacing girders and struts, and two enormous flywheels, connected to a battery of massive gears and churning pushrods.

"What the Hell is *that?*" West whispered.

The armored hull of the monstrosity rose into view, as

the shrill scream of the turbines grew ever louder. It was almost insectile in appearance, with complex sliding joints and articulations, and fairly bristled with gun ports. The main forward battery bore a strong resemblance to a Gatling, albeit a Gatling made up of six-inch naval cannon.

"Offhand," Gordon said, "I'd say it's the reason why Loveless wasn't worried about losing his land ironclad."

The thing continued to rise, as the ground-shaking thudding grew in intensity, and it became apparent to West that the machine was supported by giant metal legs that moved with a massively slow but strangely delicate precision. He counted. Three legs, four, six—

"It's a tarantula," West said. He ducked and took whatever meager cover the boulder afforded. "It is the biggest goddamn tarantula in creation." Gordon joined him in cowering.

The thing passed directly overhead, eclipsing the sun. For a moment West feared that they'd been spotted, and that one of those enormous steel feet was going to stomp him clear through the face of the Earth.

Then, with a cheery toot of its steam whistle, it moved on, down the slope, and into the next canyon.

"Oh, Lordy," Gordon said, after he'd resumed breathing. "Now *that* is impressive."

They watched the steel tarantula recede into the distance. "Hey," West pointed out. "Look where he's driving it."

Gordon grinned. "Into that blind canyon we hiked

through this morning. The fool doesn't realize he's trapped."

A moment later, Gordon's smile vanished. The steel tarantula never even broke stride. Instead the—*head*, for lack of a better word—lifted, pivoted, and brought the Gatling cannon to bear on a narrow pass between two red-rock outcroppings. The cannon erupted in a deafening cascade of explosive shells, and the rock wall sloughed away in an avalanche of dust and rubble.

The steel tarantula marched through, unhindered.

West turned to Gordon. "Nice to see an invention that actually works for a change, huh?"

CHAPTER FOURTEEN

The guard paced nervously beside the *Wanderer.* He was bored and apprehensive at the same time, which made for a strange mix of feelings.

This being a henchman to a mad scientist business was not all it was cracked up to be.

Sure, the hours were good, and the pay was decent. But those three women that were always hovering around the Doc gave him the creeps, and some of those machines in the lab scared the living Hell out of him. Come to think of it, there were days the *Doc* gave him the creeps and scared the living Hell out of him, and that maniacal laugh of his didn't help things any.

Not for the first time, the guard felt a strong desire to quit this job and go back to a line of work he understood: robbing stagecoaches.

He reached the back end of the car and saw that his

partner was standing there, hiding in the shade, sneaking a cigarette. He looked around to see if anyone else was watching, then decided, what the hell. "Howdy, Don."

The other guard looked up from lighting his cigarette. "Howdy, Rob."

Rob gestured at the cigarette. "Y'all got another one of those?"

Don tossed him the pouch of Bull Durham. "Help yourself. Papers are inside."

"Thanks." Rob pulled a rolling paper out of the tobacco pouch, formed it a trough, and shook in a dab of tobacco. Tucking the pouch under his arm, he rolled the cigarette up, licked and sealed the seam, and twisted the ends tight. "Gotta match?"

"Your face and my horse's rear end." Don chortled at his own wit, then fished a sulphur match out of his shirt pocket and flipped it to Rob. He caught the tobacco pouch on the return toss. Rob struck the match on his unshaved chin, lit the cigarette, and took a long, slow draw. He shook the match out.

"Anything happenin' on your side?" Don asked.

"Nope. How 'bout yours?"

"Nope."

Rob took another puff on his cigarette and let the smoke rise through his mustache. "You feelin' as bored as I am?"

"Worse." Don tilted his head back and blew a smoke ring.

"I seen the Doc took the *Tarantula* out for another spin."

Don shook his head wearily. "I hope he's not rustlin' more of those scrawny Navajo sheep again. God Damn, I am *sick* of mutton! Roast mutton, fried mutton, boiled mutton, baked mutton! Mutton chops, mutton ribs, leg o' mutton, mutton shoulder! Why can't he go rustle some *beef*, is what I want to know."

Rob shook his head slowly. "Sure beats the Hell out of me."

"Now you take that Amazonia," Don continued. "I'll bet you a week's pay that *she* ain't eatin' mutton."

"Yeah," Rob said, nodding. He cracked a sly smile. "Tell you what. I'll just take that Amazonia, period."

Don scoffed. "You and what army?"

Rob sighed, and went back to his cigarette.

"Say," Don said, after a spell, "You heard anything yet 'bout what happened down in Loosiana?"

Rob gave Don a sidelong glance. "What do you mean?"

"I mean, it's kinda strange, ain't it? The Doc goes down there with twenty men and the *Tortoise*, and he comes back with two prisoners and *this* shot-up pile of junk." Don slapped the stern rail of the *Wanderer*. "Then a day later Hudson comes straggling in, but not one word about anybody else." Don took one last drag on his cigarette and stubbed it out on the rear coupler. "Kinda makes you wonder, y'know?"

Rob nodded. "I'll tell you, if there's one man around here I do not trust, it's that Hudson. Sneaky bastard."

Don agreed. "I don't trust *any* of 'em. Except for me and thee, and some days I'm not so sure about thee." Don grinned, which Rob took as his cue that that was supposed to be a joke. They shared a chuckle.

"Hey," Rob said, as he dropped his cigarette butt and ground it out with his bootheel, "you remember that mine payroll we knocked off in Silverton? Wasn't that a haul?"

Don smiled. "Those were the days, my friend."

"Yeah, runnin' free, livin' large. Wouldn't it be great to do that again?"

Don was puzzled. "What do you mean?"

"I mean, quit this job. Today. Tell the Doc to take this job and shove it. Go back to workin' freelance."

Don chewed his mustache. "Well, I—no, I can't. I mean I'd really like to, but I can't."

Rob cocked his head and stared at Don. "What do you mean?"

"I mean, not without givin' two weeks' notice, anyway. My references are very important to me."

Rob started to say something in reply, but instead said, "*Ow!*" as something hard hit him in the side of the neck. It fell to the ground with a tinny clink. He stooped and looked at it. "It's a brass button," he said. "Now why in tarnation—"

And that's when Gordon's miniature gas bomb exploded.

Gordon darted out from behind a yucca plant and snatched Don's revolver from its holster. "See? *That* worked."

West grabbed Rob's revolver. "Yeah, for about two seconds." The guards started to come to life again. West cocked the revolver and laid it on the bridge of Rob's nose, which made the man go quite cross-eyed. "Gentlemen," West said, "if you're half as smart as I think you are, you'll just hold still while my partner ties you up."

"Right," Don said, as he crossed his hands behind his back.

"Wouldn't think of arguin'," Rob agreed.

Gordon produced a thin rope from somewhere and threw a quick few loops around Don's wrists. "That's kinda loose," Don said. "I could pull my hands through, if I tried." Gordon gave the rope an extra tug. "That's better," Don said approvingly. Gordon paid out about two yards of line, then gave Rob the same treatment.

"You're learnin' fast," Rob said. "That knot is definitely plenty tight enough."

Once Don's and Rob's wrists were tied, West and Gordon led them off to the side of the tracks and made them sit down, back to back. Gordon started to lash the two men together.

"Oh, don't do *this*," Don complained. "You tie us up back to back like this and we'll be free in five minutes, tops."

"He's tellin' you truly," Rob added. "I tied the guards up like this when we robbed the bank in Durango—"

"Montrose," Don corrected.

"No, it was Durango. Montrose was where you tried to shoot the lock off the strongbox and killed Jeb Reed with a ricochet."

"Did *not!* That was in Ouray, and there was a deputy snipin' at us!"

"Yeah, right. A deputy with only one bullet. Probably had to go back to town to ask the sheriff for another one."

Gordon looked at West and rolled his eyes.

"Anyway," Don said, "the point is, we were robbing this bank in Montrose—"

"Durango," Rob insisted.

"Montrose."

West crossed his eyes and stuck his tongue out.

"I'm telling you, it was Durango!"

West pressed the pistol barrel against Rob's head, such that the trajectory would carry the bullet through both of their heads provided there was no substantial matter within their crania to impede the bullet's progress, as certainly seemed to be the case.

"Arte?" West asked. "What do you say I just kill them now?"

"If it'll make them shut up, you've got my vote."

A deadly silence settled over the quartet. Don shifted uncomfortably, and cleared his throat. "Sirs? May I make a suggestion?"

"Shoot," Gordon said. Rob winced. "Not you, Jim," Gordon hastily added. Rob opened his eyes again.

"Well," Don said, "we can see that y'all are new at this. So you just go and tie us up anyway you feel like, and we'll give you our word that we won't even *try* to get loose until a good ten minutes after you've made your getaway. Fair enough?"

Gordon looked at West. West gave Gordon a look in return that said he'd never heard a loonier idea in his entire life.

"Sure," said Gordon.

"Sounds good to me," added West.

"Our horses are staked out over by the locomotive," Rob added, helpfully, as Gordon resumed tying the two men together. "I mean, they're not really *our* horses—"

"Sure they are," Don said. "We stole 'em fair and square."

"The bay is mine," Rob said. "Watch out for his left front hoof. It's a little sore."

"Thanks for the tip," West said, as he helped Gordon pull the rope tight.

"The gelding is mine," Don said. "Its name is Jessica. You have to whack it over the head every now and then to get its attention."

"I'll remember that," Gordon said, as he finished tying off the end of the rope.

Rob looked down at the knot and smiled approvingly. "Now *that* is a good strong knot. I'll have to remember that one. What's it called?"

"A running bowline," Gordon said. "Now, if you gentlemen will excuse us." He caught West by the sleeve and dragged him up the back steps of the *Wanderer,* as Don and Rob smiled and waved good-bye insofar as the ropes would allow.

"Jim," Gordon whispered, as soon as they were out of earshot. "I think we should kill those two right now. Not for ourselves, but for the sake of all humanity. *They must not be allowed to breed!*"

* * *

The inside of the parlor car looked like a nicely furnished apartment that had been recently vacated by some very bad tenants. There were broken dishes on the table, dirty pots and pans in the galley, empty wine bottles everywhere, and several large and tragic stains on the oriental rugs. Gordon gasped in horror when he saw the mess, and fought the impulse to start tidying up.

West ignored it all and went straight to the pool-cue rack. Finding the hidden button, he pressed it.

There was still some pressure left in the pneumatic system. Not enough to fully revolve the pool table, but enough to flip it to the point where West could push it the rest of the way. The weapon racks were still intact and fully laden. West dumped the gun he'd grabbed from Rob, snatched a pair of the new Colts off the rack, and loaded them.

Gordon continued forward, into the stateroom car.

West ignored Gordon and continued arming for war. There was a new double-holster *buscadero* belt in one nook; he strapped it on, lashed the tie-down straps to his legs, and filled the loops with cartridges. His trusty Greener "Street Howitzer" was right where he'd left it; he broke it open, checked to make sure the lockwork was still intact, then slipped it into his left-draw thigh holster. He loaded rifles, stuffed an extra revolver into his belt, looped bandoliers of shotshells over his shoulders, and shoved handfuls of loose cartridges into all available pockets.

When it was simply physically impossible for West to

carry another weapon or cartridge on his person, he strode forward. "Come on, Gordon! It's time to *ride!*"

The stateroom was empty.

"Er, Gordon?"

"In here, James." West continued forward, into the laboratory car. Gordon was sitting cross-legged on the floor, with his nitro cycle out and a whole lot of thin metal pipes and canvas strewn about the place. In his lap, Gordon held a large and very old-looking book.

"Gordon, I mean, it's time to ride a *horse.* You do know how to ride a horse, right?"

Gordon turned a page and nodded. "I do . . . when the situation calls for something primitive."

West's jaw dropped. "Well how about, like, *now?* When we only got a crazy killer with a sixty-foot-tall steel tarantula stompin' toward our president!"

Gordon shook his head, and turned another page. "I got thinking about this morning. You know, the reason the wasp was able to kill that tarantula was because it attacked from *above,* where the spider was vulnerable."

West grabbed Gordon's shoulder and tried to tug him to his feet. "Yeah, well the wasp had one small advantage we don't have. It could fly."

Gordon flipped a page. "*Exactly!*" Gordon jumped to his feet and pushed the book in West's face. The page he had it open to showed a bizarre, complicated, batlike mechanism.

"In 1540, Leonardo da Vinci invented a flying machine he called an ornithopter! While he never built a full-size man-carrying version, the principle is—"

West batted the book aside, grabbed Gordon by the shoulders, and shook him until his teeth rattled.

"Artemus! There is no *time* for crazy plans! We got to stick to what we're *good* at!"

Without waiting for a reply, West dragged Gordon into the stateroom and threw open the wardrobe closet.

CHAPTER FIFTEEN

Press Secretary Nussbaum was, as usual, being a pain in the neck. President Grant tolerated Nussbaum's fussing with the knot in his tie a moment longer, then waved the man way.

"We're in the middle of absolutely nowhere," Grant grumbled. "There are at best five hundred people here, and half of them are Chinese construction workers. What difference does it make if my tie is straight?"

"It's for the cameras, sir," Nussbaum said, as he picked at a tiny bit of lint on Grant's shoulder. "The camera sees everything. And what the camera sees, the world sees."

"Mathew Brady's camera saw me at Petersburg with horse manure on my boots, a cigar in my hand, and a whiskey bottle on the table," Grant growled. "I don't recall as that shook the pillars of Heaven."

Nussbaum gave up on Grant's jacket and stepped back to consider his hair. "That was then, sir. This is now. We live in an age of *electric* communications these days. Why, thanks to the miracle of transatlantic telegraphy, even people in London and Paris will know about it the instant you drive that spike!" Nussbaum shook his head disapprovingly, picked up a hairbrush, and began mapping his best approach to Grant's coiffure. "And if the president of the United States were ever to appear disheveled or unkempt—"

"Yes, I know," Grant said wearily. "Western civilization as we know it would collapse." Grant shook his head, inadvertently frustrating Nussbaum's attempts to do something about his hair. "Hell of a way to run a country, if you ask me."

There came a knock at the door of the president's private car. Grant gladly seized on the interruption as a chance to break free of Nussbaum. "Yes? Enter." The door opened, and the assistant undersecretary of something-or-other came in, escorted by a Pinkerton's detective.

"Mister President? We're ready to start."

Grant nodded. "Very good. Tell them I'll be right out." The assistant undersecretary nodded and left. Grant fended off a last attempt by Nussbaum to touch up his hair and found his hat and gloves.

"Remember, sir," Nussbaum added, "it's the laurelwood tie, and there are actually *four* golden spikes. The other three will be driven in by the territorial governor and the presidents of the Central Pacific and Union Pacific Railroads—"

"Leland Stanford?" Grant interrupted. "Leland is here? And we're going to let him *speak?*"

Nussbaum nodded. "I believe that is the plan, sir."

Grant stepped over to his desk, opened a humidor, and pulled out four cigars, which he added to the two already in his breast pocket. "It's going to be a long day," he explained.

The hot May afternoon wore on. Speeches were made, the marching band played, and the cavalry from Fort Buenaventura performed a demonstration of horsemanship that spoke volumes about why they were stationed here and not someplace where they might be seen by the public. Fortunately a light breeze was blowing, and it kept the brine flies off. Grant was down three cigars and ready to trade his soul for a shot of whiskey when his turn to speak finally came.

As he mounted the platform, Grant scanned the sweating faces in the crowd and came to a decision. There was a brilliantly written speech in his right jacket pocket, laden with homespun homilies, florid metaphors, and scintillating similes. In his read-through the night before, it had taken just slightly over an hour to deliver the speech with proper timing and full impact.

Grant looked out over the sea of faces, realized that half of them probably didn't even understand English, and decided to leave the speech in his pocket. Instead, he picked up the Golden Spike, held it in his hand as if weighing it, then looked up and smiled at the crowd.

"Damn, it's heavy." A few in the front row tittered.

Grant bit the spike, and considered the results. "Real gold, too." This brought some louder laughs.

Grant pretended to slip the spike into his coat pocket. "So thank you all for inviting me, and now if you don't mind—"

The crowd broke up in a roar of hearty laughter. When it'd calmed a bit, and Grant sensed that the tension had eased nicely, he smiled, and launched into an improvised and greatly truncated version of his speech.

He ended ten minutes later by reading the incription on the spike. When the applause and cheering died down, he added, "Now, it is my great honor to use the iron of the East, and the gold of the West, to drive this final spike, thus symbolizing the completion of this mighty railroad that spans the continent and weds the oceans!" He stepped down from the podium, walked over to the laurelwood tie, and handed the Golden Spike to Leland Stanford. Stanford crouched down and positioned the spike in the predrilled hole in the tie. Someone handed Grant a sledgehammer, and he raised it high. Stanford stepped back.

The spike fell over.

A few in the crowd snickered.

"Nice going, Leland," Grant muttered, as he lowered the hammer. Stanford darted in and set the spike up again. Grant raised the hammer one more time.

The spike popped out of the hole.

Grant lowered the hammer. "Very funny. Are we going to be doing this all day?"

Stanford blanched. "Mr. President, I assure you . . . *look!*" He pointed at the spike on the ground.

All by itself, the spike hopped an inch.

Grant was puzzled. "What the hell?"

"*Listen!*" Stanford gasped. A moment later, Grant heard it too; a deep, ponderous thumping like a steelworks drop forge; a sound that was more *felt* than heard, and it was growing louder.

Grant turned on Stanford. "I thought you gave your crews the day off. Is some fool dynamiting around—?"

"*LOOK!*" someone off to the side of the crowd screamed. Grant spun, but saw nothing except confusion. He darted up to the podium as the general panic and screaming began, and picked out another note in the discord: a shrill, piercing whine, erratic in pitch but growing in volume. The sound was almost lost in the thunder of stampeding feet and terrified voices.

Then *it* stepped into view, and Grant's jaw dropped.

The Pinkertons nearly bowled Grant over in their rush to join the fleeing crowd. The captain of the Buenaventura cavalry troop dashed up and whipped off a hasty salute. "Mister President, sir!" Grant was rooted to the spot, staring at the thing. "Mister President?" He didn't even blink.

"*General Grant!*"

Grant snapped out of it. "Yes, Captain?"

"*What should we do, sir?*"

Grant looked at the captain, looked at the machine,

looked around for an avenue of escape, and realized there was none. "Give me your saber!" he barked, as he snatched it from the captain's scabbard. "Then take cover!" The captain ran off. A massive steel foot slammed down on the ground not ten feet in front of Grant.

The giant steel spider stopped.

The silence, broken only by the slight hiss of escaping steam and the whine of the idling turbine, was terrifying.

Doctor Loveless flipped a few switches and lifted an electric speaking tube to his lips. The sound-expansion horns gave his voice the resonance of a minor god.

"Well, well, isn't this a happy coincidence! Here I am out for a little ride, and right in the middle of nowhere, I bump into General Ulysses S. Grant himself!" Loveless leaned over the edge of the flying bridge and gave Grant a mocking salute.

"We've never been properly introduced, sir! I'm Dr. Arliss Loveless, formerly of the Confederate States of America!"

Grant stuck the saber into the ground, opened his jacket, and retrieved a cigar. Coolly and calmly, he bit the end off, struck a match, and lit the cigar, rolling it until it was well and thoroughly lit.

Grant cleared his throat, as if he had all the time in the world. "Yes, Dr. Loveless. What can I do for you today?" From the corners of his eyes, he noticed the cavalry captain quietly moving his men into flanking positions.

Loveless lifted the speaking tube again. *"I have a humble abode nearby, and I was hoping you'd accept my hos-*

pitality! Some friends and I have a little proposition we'd like to present!"

Grant drew on his cigar, looked thoughtful, and blew out a stream of smoke. "I'm not sure. My schedule is quite booked up at the moment. What kind of proposition did you have in mind?"

"The complete, unconditional, and immediate surrender of the United States of America!"

Grant seemed puzzled. "Surrender? I didn't realize that we were at war with anyone."

Loveless nodded to Munitia. The Gatling cannon swung into action and spit a burst of explosive shells at one of the locomotives on the track below. The locomotive was instantly blasted to flaming scrap, and the people who'd taken shelter behind both trains ran screaming.

Loveless giggled.

"How about now, Mr. President?" Loveless leaned over the edge of the flying bridge and looked down.

There were two President Grants.

Two *absolutely identical* President Grants.

"In matters of war," the left one said, "the person to talk to would be me."

Loveless dropped his speaking tube. He looked around the bridge, probing for an answer. Amazonia shrugged. Munitia shook her head. Lippenreider pantomimed that she didn't have her opera glasses with her.

Loveless found both his voice and his speaking tube again. *"Now, just who are you, sir?"*

"Tell him I'm the president," Gordon whispered.

"He's the president," Grant said.

"Then who have I been speaking with?"

Gordon turned to Grant and snorted dismissively. "Him? He's an actor, hired to stand in for me on public occasions. A rather *bad* actor, I must admit. A little puffy and over-weight."

Grant puffed nervously on his cigar and eyed Gordon narrowly, unsure of whether he liked where this was going. Gordon in turn puffed vigorously on *his* cigar and eyed Grant, *obviously* displeased with the way things were going.

Grant took the cigar out of his mouth, and whispered, "You've got a lot of brass, Gordon, I'll give you that. Where's West?"

"You know him, sir." Gordon shifted his eyes. As unob-trusively as possible, Grant followed Gordon's line of sight.

West had circled around behind the destroyed train and was running silently toward one of the back legs of the *Tarantula*. He reached it undetected and started to climb.

Gordon turned to the cavalry officer. "Captain, get this impostor out of my sight! His pathetic attempts at imper-sonation sicken me!" Puzzled and hesitant, the Buenaven-tura cavalry officer emerged from hiding and started to lead Grant away. Suddenly Grant stopped, snatched the saber out of the ground, and looked defiantly up at Loveless.

"*I* am the president of the United States! *That* man is the impostor! And *you*, sir, are a haunchless swine!"

Gordon was stunned by Grant's unexpected move to up-stage him. He stepped forward and raised his voice. "I say again, I am Grant!" Aside, he said to Grant, "Sir, what are you doing? We're trying to get you out of here."

Grant shook his head. "Diversionary tactic. I'll confuse Loveless and buy West more time." Both of them looked across. West was already halfway up the leg.

To a certain extent, Grant had succeeded, and Loveless was confused. It didn't last long, though. "Munitia!" he barked. "Shoot them both! We'll sort it out later!" Munitia, manning a sort of swivel cannon, took a steady bead on Grant and Gordon and began to squeeze the trigger —

"**U**h-oh," Gordon said.

A stream of sticky white synthetic spider silk shot out of the barrel of Munitia's cannon, enveloping both Grant and Gordon. Grant had just time enough to turn to Gordon, and say, "Getting caught in a giant spider's web is part of your plan, right?"

Gordon could only blink. "I'm by your side, sir. That's the important part."

Loveless nodded. Munitia shut off the web cannon and threw a switch. A small winch began to turn, taking in the silk and hoisting Grant and Gordon off the ground —

BLAM! A bullet split the silken cord and dropped the two men roughly but safely back to earth.

"*Where did that come from?*" Loveless demanded. "Munitia! Amazonia!" He twisted helplessly in his chair, trying to see something. "Can anyone—?"

"There, sir," Lippenreider said, pointing. "On the port quarter leg. It's—" Her jaw dropped.

"*Gott in Himmel!* It's West!"

Loveless flushed red with outrage. "*MUNITIA!*"

"On it, sir." She jumped to a gun mount. Amazonia took a Gatling. Lippenreider dashed below decks. Unnoticed by the crew of the *Tarantula*, the cavalry troop on the ground below raised up their carbines and took aim.

And then a fair approximation of all hell broke loose.

Jim West never stood a chance. He fought bravely; he fought ferociously. He nearly made it to the lower deck of the *Tarantula*. But the ricochets from the cavalry rifles were almost as dangerous as the aimed fire from Loveless's crew, while the leg girders offered only meager protection. In the end, it was a story of revolvers against machine guns.

A bullet struck him full in the chest. West slipped, almost recovered, then lost his grip and plummeted to the ground below. He hit the dirt like a nerveless bag of meat and lay terribly, terribly still.

"Well," Loveless said cheerfully, "it's about bloody time. Munitia! Collect the presidents. Amazonia! Set course for home." Loveless leaned over the edge of the flying bridge and saluted his fallen foe.

"Captain West? This has been great fun, and I look forward to killing you again in your next life!"

CHAPTER SIXTEEN

An uneasy quiet settled over the Promontory Mountains. The railroad-construction crews huddled in their camps, arguing in six languages over whether it was smarter to pull out now or wait until morning. The survivors of the Buenaventura cavalry troop withdrew to the east, hoping to pick up reinforcements and artillery before risking another run-in with the *Tarantula*. Press Secretary Nussbaum gave up trying to find a working telegraph line, and instead called a staff meeting in an overturned boxcar, where he and the few officials he could round up assertively discussed options and got exactly nowhere. Four Pinkerton agents turned in their resignations, effective immediately. The shattered wreck of the No. 119 locomotive at last burned out.

Jim West's body lay stiff and unmoving, exactly where it had fallen two hours before. A line of forager ants moved across his face, prospecting for food. One ant explored his right nostril but found nothing there of interest. Another took a shortcut across the dry, glazed surface of West's unseeing right eye. A brine fly landed in the gash on West's head, searching for moisture, but the blood was long since dried to a brown crust.

Overhead, vultures circled. . . .

Gordon was somewhat surprised to find himself still alive. After returning to Spider Canyon it'd taken Loveless less than a minute to identify the real Grant, and Amazonia had been none too gentle when she'd removed Gordon's fake beard and nose. But after that they'd settled for merely binding his wrists with a pair of heavy iron manacles and tossing him headfirst into a dank stone cell, and when he'd regained conciousness, he found he was sharing accommodations with Coleman, and that Rita and the surviving kidnapped scientists were in the adjoining cells. No one else there knew any more than Gordon did, and most of them knew considerably less. Two of the bearded and bedraggled scientists were no longer even certain of their own names.

After that, the conversation petered out quickly, and there was nothing to do but sit in the dark and listen to the rats scurry. An unguessed span of time later, Amazonia returned, this time wearing a tight brown quasi-military outfit and accompanied by a goon squad in matching uniforms. Gordon, Coleman, Rita, and the rest were released from their cells, but not from their manacles, and escorted at gunpoint to an upper level. Through a window along the way Gordon caught a glimpse of deep blue sky, and guessed that it was near sunset. They passed through a great bronze double door, and into an amphitheater.

The amphitheater took Gordon's breath away.

Not because it was attractive; no, far from it. And while it certainly wasn't the *ugliest* room he'd ever played—that honor was forever held by an opera house in Cleveland that was simply infested with obese gilded cherubs—it was definitely a top contender for second place. The room was some kind of ghastly overdone neo-Romanesque mausoleum, decorated with a profusion of colorful banners and faux heraldry, and it had the ambient acoustics of an empty barn. The room was also filled with a milling throng of people, and as Gordon advanced into the room, he began to recognize faces. Most of them were Europeans who'd been at Loveless's party in New Orleans.

One other man's face was a welcome sight: President Grant, who seemed a bit rumpled but otherwise none the worse for wear.

Amazonia led Gordon and the other prisoners over to Grant, handed them off to the guards, and went to join Munitia and Lippenreider. Gordon tried to talk to Grant, and received a rap on the head from a guard for his trouble.

The lights dimmed dramatically. The band struck up a tune: some kind of heavy Germanic march that Gordon immediately hated. The music was overflowing with *Sturm und Drang* and way too many descant trumpets and cymbals crashes, and sadly short on melody and pleasing qualities. It sounded like—well, like music to goosestep to. Amazonia and Lippenreider seemed very pleased.

The great double doors swung open again, and Loveless rolled into the room: smiling, ebullient. He had traded his white operetta admiral's uniform for a black military tunic festooned with golden epaulettes and gaudy medals, and on his head he wore a Prussian coalscuttle helmet, complete with horsehair crest. Amazonia, Munitia, and Lippenreider took up their stations and followed a respectful three paces behind as Loveless rolled through the room, meeting and greeting the foreign dignitaries.

The martial music came to a climax and, thankfully, died dramatically, as Loveless completed his circuit of the room and rolled up onto the stage. There, framed by a large black flag featuring a highly stylized spider emblem, he turned to the crowd and raised his arms expansively.

"*Bonjour!*" Loveless called out. "*Welkommen! Buenas tardes*, and good day! *Great*, victorious day! Let me welcome my distaff warriors, my friends, and my distinguished guests!" He smiled broadly as he surveyed the room, then zeroed in on Gordon.

"I think we're all here. At least, everyone who is going to make it in *this* lifetime. . . ."

The vulture coasted in for landing next to West's body. A graceful, soaring creature in the air, it moved with clumsy hops on the ground, and cocked its grotesque and featherless head quizzically. This man-thing in the dirt seemed to be quite, completely, and irrevocably dead. Yummy. The buzzard leaned closer, its breath stinking and hot on West's face. . . .

West's fist flashed out in blind reflex. "Get *off* me!" The buzzard went sprawling, then flew away in a flurry of terrified squawking. West sat up like he'd been electrified, and lashed out blindly again, hands slapping at his face. "Off! Get away! Aaaah! *Bugs!* Get 'em off me, get 'em off, get 'em—"

Abruptly, West realized that he was conscious. More surprisingly, he was alive. He felt his head. It hurt like hell and he'd have a lump the size of a goose egg in the morning, but the cut had stopped bleeding. He'd had worse.

Bits of memory began to fill in, like a jigsaw puzzle completing itself. He remembered the *Tarantula*. He remembered Grant and Gordon, caught in the web. He remembered a gunfight.

He clearly remembered getting shot.

It was a good hit, too. Center chest. Right in the heart. Heavy caliber. He should be as dead as dead gets by now. Afraid of what he might find, at first, then more frightened by what he might *not* find, West grabbed his chest.

His heart was beating, good. He tried an experimental deep breath. The lungs seemed to be working too. He could feel that he had a good bruise on his sternum, but otherwise no obvious damage. No blood; no broken bones. He began exploring more carefully now. There was a ragged hole in his jacket, right exactly where he remembered the bullet striking home.

West looked down, and began unbuttoning his jacket, then his vest. The outer layer of fabric was destroyed. But the *inner* layer didn't look the way he remembered it. It had a strange, metallic, sheen, and a weird kind of over-lapping-scale pattern. West had seen that pattern like that before, and tried to place it. It reminded him of —

Gordon's *Impermeable Waistcoat.*

Strangely, West's first reaction was to howl. "*Artemus! I told you not to mess with my stuff!*"

Gordon was beginning to think that death *would* be preferable to having to listen to another five minutes of Loveless's speech. "Finally," Loveless said . . .

("*At last,*" Gordon muttered, which earned him an-other whack from the guard.)

". . . the glorious moment we've all been waiting for. Some of us for a *very* long time." Loveless looked to the English ambassador. "Seventeen-seventy six, wasn't it, old bean? Most expensive cup of tea in history!" As the rest of the audience clapped and smiled, the Englishman nodded soberly.

"The months I spent on your continent recuperating from my wounds were a time of great enlightenment for me," Loveless continued, amazingly long-winded for someone with only one lung. "I came to see America from your perspective—as home to some of the greatest hucksters, swindlers, and crooked horse traders in the his-tory of the world!" He turned to Hudson. "Manhattan for a handful of beads, *kemosabe?*" Loveless raised his open hand, dropped his voice to a basso falsetto, and grunted, *"How."*

He turned to the Mexican delegation. "Remember the Alamo? Indeed!"

Turning to face the crowd again, Loveless removed his Prussian helmet and lowered his eyes, feigning humility. "Today, my friends, I come before you to tell you that the wrongs will be righted . . . the past, made present . . . the injustices, undone . . . and the united, once more, divided!" He made a grand, sweeping gesture. "Behold!"

To the thunderous applause of the audience, the flag behind Loveless was pulled down, to reveal a map of —

"The De-United States," Grant read out loud. "This does not look good."

Loveless waved his arms to quiet the crowd and eventually got control of the room again. "As you can see, we've made a few *improvements*! Great Britain gets back her original thirteen colonies—minus Manhattan, of course!"

The British ambasssador stood, and gravely acknowledged the round of applause.

"Florida and the Fountain of Youth go back to Spain!"

The Spaniards stood and accepted the accolades.

"Texas, New Mexico, California, and Arizona return to Mexico!" The Mexicans stood, and Loveless pointed to them. "Of course, you'll have to work out your own differences with Spain. I can't solve *everyone's* problems, you know!" This line got a mixture of applause and laughter.

"To France, the Louisiana Purchase!" The French War Minister and "Marie Antoinette" stood, and took a bow.

"And the rest," Loveless added impishly, "is just a tiny little homestead on which *I* can retire." The crowd laughed appreciatively as Munitia pulled a string and the names of Colorado, Utah, Kansas, and Nevada fell away, to be replaced by "Loveless Land."

"This does *not* look good," Grant repeated.

West stumbled aboard the unguarded *Wanderer*. He wasn't entirely sure how he'd covered the miles from Promontory Point to Spider Canyon so quickly, but the more he thought about the events that had transpired since he'd fallen off the leg of the *Tarantula*, the more he realized that he didn't want to think about them. Instead, as his eyes adjusted to the dim light inside the parlor car, it became quite clear to him why the car was no longer guarded.

The place had been ransacked. Every last weapon had been removed, every drawer dumped out, every secret panel pried open and emptied. Even Professor Morton's head was gone from the icebox. All that remained were Gordon's cycle, the collection of random junk in the work room, and Gordon's wardrobe closet.

Gordon's wardrobe closet.

West reached into the back of the closet and felt around until he found a certain wide belt with a singularly large silver buckle. He examined the buckle a moment, then tapped it just so. The buckle sprang open and deposited a loaded derringer into West's waiting hand.

West lifted the tiny gun and considered it. A .41 rimfire. A belly gun, that was accurate to maybe ten feet. A *popgun*, that he wouldn't normally use on a gopher, for fear that it would only leave the poor critter wounded and suffering.

There has to be a better way . . .

Gordon could only sit there and shake his head. *It must be a universal principle*, he thought. *Writers always secretly believe they're actors. Actors always secretly believe they're singers. And sawed-off little sadistic megalomaniacs?*

The "anthem" that was being brayed throughout the room limped to a painfully bombastic and drawn-out close. Loveless lowered his baton and rewarded the assembled multitude with a smile. "Did you enjoy that? I penned the lyrics myself." The question got a sort of murmured, vaguely positive response from the crowd, though Gordon could see that many of the Europeans were covertly crumpling up the sheet music, dropping it to the floor, and stepping on it.

Loveless turned to President Grant.

"Well, ladies and gentlemen, I'm afraid we've reached the end of the entertainment portion of this evening's program, so it's time for the moment you've all been waiting for. President Grant, *come on down!*" Loveless snapped his fingers.

Hudson and another goon dragged a desk and a chair out to center stage. Another two guards seized Grant by the upper arms, frog-marched him over to the desk, and forced him to sit in the chair. Hudson placed a pen in Grant's manacled hands.

Loveless smiled.

"President Grant? My partner nations insist that we make this transition of power as legal as humanly possible. Personally, I also appreciate the symmetry of the event. After all, wasn't it you who made Lee surrender at Appomattox?"

Loveless turned to the crowd. "Ladies and gentlemen: the *surrender order!*" With a dramatic flourish and to general applause, he unrolled the paper and laid it on the desk before Grant. A hush fell over the room.

"Sign here, please."

Grant dropped the pen and sat back. "I will not."

"You don't understand. You have no choice."

Insofar as the handcuffs allowed, Grant resolutely crossed his arms across his chest. "Never will I sign that piece of paper. Never will the United States surrender!"

Loveless pursed his lips and shook his head. "Never say never, Mr. Grant. Either you sign these Articles of Surrender, or I will have you shot." This unsporting threat brought an undercurrent of dismayed looks and muttering from the audience.

Go for it, Arliss! Gordon thought. *Your audience is turning on you! Go ahead, make 'em walk out in the third act!*

Grant stood up and kicked back his chair. "Do your worst, Loveless. I have put my life on the line for my country before, and I will be proud to do it again."

Loveless stroked his chin, and reconsidered. "You

would, wouldn't you? But how brave are you when someone *else* is in the line of fire? Someone who works for you, and trusts you.

"Let's up the ante, shall we? Either you sign that surrender order right now, or I shall shoot . . . *Gordon!*" Loveless whirled and nodded to Amazonia, who dragged the president back to his seat and grabbed Gordon instead.

Rita jumped to her feet. "Artemus!"

Gordon winked at her. "Don't worry," he whispered as he passed Grant, "I'm wearing an Impermeable Waistcoat." But there was no time for further explanation as Amazonia hauled him up to the stage. Hudson produced a rifle from somewhere and took aim.

Gordon held up one finger—his left index finger. "Dr. Loveless, may I have one last request?"

Loveless motioned for Hudson to hold off a moment. "And that would be?"

"Would you please instruct your hired killer to aim for my heart . . . which has loved this great country so much!"

Loveless considered the request. "Not a chance, Mr. Gordon. Hudson, shoot him in the head."

Gordon's bold smile sagged. "Great."

"Ready!" Loveless barked out. A drumroll began, and Hudson cocked his rifle. "Aim!" Hudson leveled the rifle and took a steady bead on Gordon's forehead.

Loveless turned to Grant. "There's still time to save Gordon's life."

"Never!" Grant shouted back. "He'll get a posthumous Medal of Honor for this!"

("Thank you, Mister President," Gordon muttered.)

"Then may his blood be on your hands! Mr. Hudson—"

The crowd gasped.

The room was plunged into blackout.

A single white spotlight flared on, and swept across to stage right. The drumroll resolved into a flam and a rimshot.

And *she* stood there, glorious, beautiful, and utterly radiant in that slinky sequined blue dress. Hudson, confused, lowered his rifle and looked to Loveless for instructions, but Loveless was simply staring bug-eyed at the tall black woman. The bass drum counted three *largo* as she sashayed across the stage, twirling her feather boa, then the band rolled into a wonderfully sleazy, bluesy, intro. . . .

"*Oooh, Hangtown girls are plump and rosy,*" the chanteuse sang, in a husky voice that bespoke too much whiskey and sex.

Loveless's jaw dropped.

"*Hair in ringlets, might cosy . . .*"

Hudson took aim at Gordon's head again, then realized Loveless had forgotten all about the execution, and snorted in disgust and uncocked the rifle. Gordon resumed breathing.

"*Painted cheeks and frilly corsets . . .*"

She stopped next to Loveless's chair, did a bump and grind, and struck a coquettish pose with hands clasped and derrière out. Loveless grabbed her butt, and she slapped him.

"Touch them and they'll sting like hornets!"

The crowd gasped and Amazonia took a protective step closer to Loveless, but he merely laughed. "Ebonia, my love, why are you so cruel to me?" She blew him a kiss and sauntered away.

"Oh, Hangtown girls are lovely creatures . . ."

Hey, Gordon suddenly realized, *I have a dress like that! But, no, that* can't *be!*

"Think they'll marry Mormon preachers . . ."

Ebonia threw her feather boa around Amazonia's neck, which drew a surprisingly pleased reaction from the large blonde woman, and thus Amazonia completely failed to notice that Ebonia was picking her pockets.

"Heads thrown back, to show their features . . ."

Ebonia slipped the handcuff keys to Coleman, who by now had figured out what was really going on, then wrapped herself around Gordon and pretended to nuzzle up to his ear.

("Coleman has the keys," West whispered. "How am I doing?")

("Completely over the top," Gordon answered. "But look, there's something you need to know about that dress.")

("Later. Gotta go. Big finish.") West pressed the Derringer into Gordon's hands and slinked away. Gordon slipped the gun up his sleeve.

"Oh wo ohhhh, Hangtown girls!"

The audience instantly leapt to their feet, applauding

and whistling wildly. Amazonia blew Ebonia a big, wet kiss. Coleman took advantage of the noise and excitement to unlock himself and Rita, then pass the key to Grant. Grant looked down at the keys in surprise. "Where did you get these?" he whispered.

Coleman nodded at Ebonia. "From Captain West."

Rita overheard, and her eyes bugged out. "She's . . . *no!*"

Ebonia bowed, curtsied, waved, smiled to the audience, and tried to exit stage right, but someone started shouting *"Encore!"* and pretty soon they dragged her back. The band members, enjoying themselves for the first time this evening, counted a fast four and broke into a new song, and Ebonia rose to the bait.

> *"Oh, your weevily wheat isn't fit to eat,*
> *and neither is your barley . . .*
> *We'll have the best of Boston wheat,*
> *to bake a cake for Charley . . ."*

Suddenly West stopped, blinked, and said, "Wait a minute! What the *Hell* am I doing?" But even though he'd stopped, the tassels on his bosom were still spinning like propellers. The musicians screeched to a halt—

West's breasts exploded, in two blasting thermite flares. He spun around to shout a question at Gordon, and accidentally incinerated Hudson in the process. Amazonia was still wishing that *she* had a dress like that when the pieces clicked together in Loveless's hormone-fogged brain.

"Kill him!" Loveless shrieked.

"Who?"

"Him! Him!" Loveless pointed. "The *girl*!" A half dozen of Loveless's goons rushed West.

Coleman leaped to his feet, smashed a guard in the face with his manacles, and snatched the man's rifle as he went down. He snapped off three quick shots at the men attacking West, dropping two in their tracks, and pretty much turning the crowd in the room into a screaming, stampeding melee. Tables were overturned, china and crystal crashed to the floor, and Loveless's praetorian guard began to fire wildly and indiscriminately at pretty much anything moving.

Coleman made it to Gordon, smashed the skull of his guard with the rifle butt, and dragged him behind cover. West, his breasts smoking and burned out, joined them a moment later.

"*Where's Loveless?*" West demanded, as Coleman unlocked Gordon's cuffs.

"*Where's Grant?*" Gordon demanded, as Coleman emptied the rifle at more of their attackers.

"*He's getting away!*" West shouted, pointing at Loveless, who with his entourage was exiting through a round steel vault door.

"*Amazonia is carrying the president!*" Gordon wailed.

"And I am out of ammo," Coleman pointed out. "So unless you've got something else up your . . . sleeve, Captain West . . ."

"I got *this*." West pulled a pool ball out from under his

petticoats, thumbed the number spot, and lobbed it over-hand at the nearest group of Loveless's henchmen.

"*Not the* eight *ball!*" Gordon shrieked. He hit the floor and covered his head with his hands.

KA-BOOOM!!!!

Gordon picked himself up off the floor, brushed the dust and debris off his jacket, and started looking for a path through the raging inferno formerly known as an amp-itheatre. "Rita!"

West grabbed his elbow. "She's okay, Arte. Look. See?" He pointed through the smoke and flames, and Gordon saw that Rita and the scientists were on the far-side of the room, scrambling out through a newly opened hole in the wall.

Coleman joined them. "I'd say we've brought this party to a successful conclusion, gentlemen, but Loveless still has the President. What do you propose we do?"

The *Tarantula* thudded across the desert, turbines screaming, stacks belching flame. Loveless's hair whipped wildly in the cool night breeze. Grant was bruised, battered, and handcuffed to the superstructure, but still wide-awake and full of fight.

"You don't get it, do you?" Loveless shouted at Grant. "With this machine I don't *need* an army, and I don't *need* those mewling fools who called themselves my allies! With this machine I can rule the world!"

"And *you* don't realize, Dr. Loveless, that this contraption is still a poor excuse for brains and legs." Grant twisted into a mule kick and booted Amazonia in the behind, sending her flying.

Loveless only laughed. "What a *pathetic* response, Mr. President! And now, I'm going to demonstrate why you're wrong.

"Munitia! Set course for Silverado!"

CHAPTER SEVENTEEN

Coleman, Gordon, and West made it back to the *Wanderer* without picking up either company or opposition. Coleman found a lantern in the tender and got it going, and was immediately devastated to find out what had become of his pet engine.

"The Vandals!" he moaned, tracing a finger over a shattered gauge. "The half-crazed Visigoths! They've *ruined* her!" A tear trickled down his weathered cheek.

"Take it easy," West said, as he patted Coleman on the shoulder. "We stop Loveless, and we'll have all the time in the world to make the *Wanderer* good as new." His expression turned deadly serious. "We don't stop Loveless, and it won't matter."

Gordon returned from his exploration of the parlor car. "They've picked it clean," he announced. "Taken everything that could be removed, and smashed the rest."

West shook his head. "Only the weapons."

Gordon cocked an eyebrow. "Oh? And what exactly do you suggest that we fight with, then?"

West smiled. "Settle down, Gordon. I'm surprised at you. Y'see, damn near getting killed today taught me a lesson. Maybe it's more important to use our *brains* 'stead of our weapons, and maybe it's not such a bad idea to have some kind of *plan* worked out before we go charging in, guns blazing and all. And *you*, my friend, are just *full* of brains and plans."

Gordon really didn't know what to say. The idea of being complimented by West had simply never occurred to him before.

"So tell me: that flying machine idea of yours. Were you just *acting* like you knew what you were talking about, or do you think you can actually *build* the thing?"

The struts went together surprisingly fast. Stitching together the twenty yards of canvas was another matter.

"Now," Gordon explained, "Bernoulli's principle states that the air flowing over the top surface of a wing is moving at a lower pressure than the air moving under the wing, and this air-pressure imbalance creates a force that we call *lift*."

West horsed the wing strut into place on the spar and started fumbling with a stove bolt. "Gordon," he said between grunts of exertion, "I need to *fly* this thing, not fall asleep!"

Coleman lit another cigarette and studied the engine,

which now sported a large propeller. "It burns *what?*" he asked again.

"A volatile aromatic liquid hydrocarbon called benzene," Gordon explained, "enhanced with other chemicals, principally nitromethane."

"And you say there's no steam in it at all?"

"Absolutely none," Gordon said proudly.

Coleman scratched his head. "I just cannot understand how you claim to get all that horsepower out of such tiny pistons. Could you go over this so-called internal-combustion process just one more time?"

"Certainly," Gordon agreed. "There are actually four phases of the power cycle."

"Guys?" West said, as he wrestled with an unwieldy aileron.

"During the first phase, or 'intake' stroke—"

"*GUYS!*"

Gordon and Coleman turned to West. "Yes?" Gordon said.

"If you and Mr. Wizard could sidetrack your discussion for a while, I could sure use some *help* here."

"Sorry." Gordon darted in to help West secure the last set of bolts, while Coleman returned to the makeshift worktable he'd set up. A few minutes later West and Gordon had the flying machine finished, as far as they could tell without actually trying it, and Coleman had returned with a half dozen hand-sized canisters.

"Here's a coupla bon voyage presents, boys," Coleman said.

West eyed the canisters suspiciously. "What are they?"

"Oh, just a few common household chemicals, mixed together in the proper proportions. They're perfectly safe as long as you don't drop them."

Gordon accepted a cannister and held it gingerly. "And what happens if you drop them?"

Coleman smiled. "Why don't you let Loveless discover that?"

Gordon gratefully albeit nervously, accepted the rest of the grenades, and stuffed them into his jacket pockets. He finished and looked up to find West sitting in the saddle of the flying machine.

"What do you think you're doing, Jim?"

"Driving, Arte."

"This is *my* nitro-cycle you are sitting on. I will fly it."

Coleman shook his head in exasperation. "Will *one* of you children please fly it?"

West looked at Coleman, looked at Gordon, and without further comment, climbed out of the pilot's saddle and let Gordon take the controls. Gordon took a moment to polish his goggles, opened the fuel-line petcock, engaged the magneto, and rested his foot on the starter pedal.

"*AVANT!*"

The machine raced across the rough desert ground, gaining speed but not altitude. It crow-hopped a few times, each time landing with a bone-crunching jolt, but showed no signs of wanting to stay airborne.

"Too much weight!" Gordon shouted. "We're not getting enough lift!"

West gave him an encouraging pat. "You can do it, Arte!"

"I've got an idea!" Gordon veered sharply left.

"Uh, Gordon?" West asked. "We're heading for a cliff, you know that, right?"

"Yes! When we go off the cliff, the added velocity from the fall will give us the additional lift we need to achieve . . ."

West's eyes bugged out. "GORDON!" They ran off the edge of the cliff.

They flew.

"It worked!" Gordon crowed. "It actually *worked*!"

West looked down at the ground, which was already far below, and slapped Gordon on the back. "Arte, if you had to get one invention right, I'm sure glad it was this one."

Gordon wasn't listening to West, though. He was still reeling with exhiliration. *It worked!* He twisted the throttle open, raced the engine up to maximum power, and threw the flying machine into a steeply banking turn. "*YEEE-HAAAAA!*"

West just grinned. "I'll make a cowboy out of you yet, Arte!"

About a half mile outside of Silverado, Loveless slowed the *Tarantula*. It was a pretty town, Grant decided, as he watched the tiny lights of Main Street twinkle in the deepening purple twilight. Picturesque, in a rough-hewn and rustic way, like so many of these Western towns—a collage of wooden frame buildings, livery stables, dry goods stores, homes, and saloons. There was a tall white church steeple at one end of town and a brightly lit whorehouse at the other, offering the residents a clear choice between Heaven and Hell, and even at this distance the laughter and tinny piano music made it clear which way the townsfolk were leaning. There also appeared to be a low adobe jail or sheriff's office near the south end of town, and what looked to be about a five-hundred-gallon water tower near the train station, but beyond that, the town offered nothing that looked even remotely like fire- or Indian-fighting equipment.

Grant's heart sank, and he felt a terrible weight upon his shoulders. One incendiary shell, and the town of Silverado would go up like a heap of straw and matchsticks.

Loveless backed his wheelchair away from the control console, turned to Grant, and offered the surrender document again. "One last chance, Mister President. Sign the surrender order now, or I will decimate this town."

Grant shook his head. "You already have my answer. The United States will never yield to terror."

Loveless frowned. "Then these deaths are on your head." He beckoned for Amazonia to come up to the bridge. She brought a tray of cotton balls. Loveless selected two, and stuffed them into his ears. "I find the sound of innocent victims screaming as they are blown to pieces ruins the ear for fine music, Mr. President. Don't you agree?"

Grant scowled and slapped the tray away. "You forget: I've heard that crap you call music."

Loveless shrugged. "Your loss." He turned to his crew. "Are we within range?"

Munitia reported back. "Yes, sir."

"Very well. Advance, and *open fire!*"

The *Tarantula* lurched into forward motion again. Loveless yanked a handle, and a steam whistle like a great screeching bird split the air. The machine's forward battery opened up with a deafening concussion, and Grant's stomach churned as he watched the first volley of shells arc into town and explode in puffs of orange flame in the center of Main Street.

Grant closed his eyes, listened to the echoes of the shell bursts, and wished for a glass of strong whiskey. Even without seeing it, he knew what was happening in the town. The *prairie dog reflex*, George Custer had called it. At the first sign of danger, at the first sound of an explosion, ordinary civilians would dash out into the streets en masse, craning their necks and hoping to see what was going on. Whereupon the second volley of shells would catch them out in the open and turn Main Street into a ghastly, blood-spattered charnel house.

Grant wished again for a shot of strong whiskey. Then he remembered how General Halleck used to criticize him for drinking after battles. *Henry, you pedantic old fool*, Grant thought. *How can you witness horror like this and not want a stiff drink?*

Grant opened his eyes. The *Tarantula* was very nearly in town, now; near enough for him to see the frantic and terrified people silhouetted against the flames. The cannons belched and flamed; the Gatlings chattered; innocent people screamed and died. The saloon and several other Main Street buildings were already fully engulfed in flames, and the roof of the livery stable was catching. There were twisted dark lumps lying everywhere in the streets; they were the dead, or the dying.

The forward turret pivoted and fired something new. It was a complicated gun mount that seemed to belch out fireballs and spit streams of brilliant liquid fire. The upper floors of the hotel exploded into an instant inferno, while flaming debris fell on the mob in the street below.

Bile rose in Grant's throat. Unbidden, a memory came back to him: the Battle of the Wilderness. The artillery there had ignited a forest fire, and the Union and Confederate armies slugged it out in short, savage, hand-to-hand battles amidst the smoke and flames. Twenty-five thousand men died that day, and most of the wounded burned to death.

A shrill, inhuman scream rent the air, and brought Grant back to the here and now. Grant *knew* that sound, and it made his skin crawl. It was the sound of a horse dying.

Grant's soldier's soul *begged* for whiskey, as his rational mind fought for detachment. He thought of the Bloody Angle in Spotsylvania, where the ground was carpeted with layers of Union and Confederate dead. He thought of Vicksburg, after three months of Union shelling, and compared it to the destruction the *Tarantula* had wrought in mere minutes.

On another level, he was impressed.

Shots spanged harmlessly off the machine's lower hull. The Gatling crews answered with lethal swiftness. *Run away!* Grant thought. *You can't fight this thing with Winchesters!*

Or maybe you can, Grant reconsidered, at last finding a hook to hang his sanity on. *If I were in command on the ground, how would I fight this thing?* Like a well-oiled machine, his West Point–trained tactical mind clicked into gear, and Grant's grief and horror were shunted aside.

There's no point trying to punch through the hull—at least, not with anything short of an eight-inch siege gun. But the upper deck seems relatively thin and unprotected. Perhaps a high-angle weapon, like a mortar or a howitzer . . .

Suddenly sharp-eyed and analytical, Grant began studying everything he could see of the bridge and upper deck. *It may be deadly, but it's only a machine, designed and built by humans. It* must *have a weakness.*

Gordon banked into a graceful turn. "There it is!" West shouted, pointing down at the *Tarantula*, which was silhouetted by many raging fires. "Let's get him! Go down there!"

"We can't just 'go down there,'" Gordon explained. "This machine depends on *lift*, and any descent must be a carefully calibrated and managed—"

"Just shut up and go down there, will ya?" West reached past Gordon and shoved the control stick forward. The machine pitched over into a screaming dive, and Gordon struggled to regain control and keep the wings from shearing off. . . .

Loveless surveyed the flaming inferno that was once a town, then unlocked Grant's handcuffs and presented him with a pen. "Well, Mr. President, has this been a sufficient demonstration? Will you now sign the surrender agreement, or must I continue on to another target—say, Denver? Wichita? St. Louis, perhaps?"

Grant shook his head and opened his mouth to speak. Whatever he said, it was lost in the noise as Gordon's flying machine suddenly came screaming out of the sky and raced not ten feet overhead. The blast from the propeller flattened Grant's hair. Two massive explosions shattered the Gatling cannon mount, and flames and warning horns erupted in a maddening cacophony.

Loveless screamed. "WHAT IN THE SACRED NAME OF STONEWALL JACKSON WAS *THAT?*"

Grant squinted at the shape as it banked into a broad turn. "I'll be damned!" he said. "It's West and Gordon on a flying machine!" He turned to Loveless. "I will now accept *your* immediate and unconditional surrender, you sawed-off bastard!"

"Never!" Loveless rolled over to the railing. "Amazonia! Munitia! Shoot them down!"

Munitia pounded a fist on her gun mount in frustration. "We're *trying* to! But the guns won't elevate high enough!"

"We designed our weapons to attack *ground* targets!" Amazonia added. "We never thought we'd have to shoot *up*!"

Grant smirked at Loveless. "Gotcha, you little rodent."

Loveless scowled. "Don't be so sure." He thought for a moment, then roughly shoved Grant out of the way and rolled over to the control panel. Pushing this lever, pulling

that handle, punching those buttons; the *Tarantula* seemed
to rouse itself from its mechanical torpor and take a hesitant step, then drop to the knees of its forward legs, pitch-
ing the stern high in the air.

"*Amazonia?*"

She swung her Gatling around. "I can aim up now, sir!"

"Good! Blast them out of the sky!" He turned to his
other surviving crew member. "Munitia, I'm through with
diplomacy. Take Grant belowdecks and *kill* him!"

Gordon was banking around for another bombing run
when a stream of .50-caliber bullets tore through the flying machine's cloth-covered wings. Gordon fought the
impact and somehow twitched the machine out of the line
of fire and kept it aloft, but a second burst of fire shattered
the starboard wing spar and sent the machine spinning out
of control.

West clung to a strut and screamed in Gordon's ear.
"Did da Vinci ever say anything about *landing* this bird?"

"I don't think he thought it would work," Gordon
said as he tried desperately to stabilize the plunge, "so
he didn't get that far. I'm open to suggestions."

"Take out as many of the bad guys as you can."

Gordon nodded and tried to steer the dying aircraft into
a suicide plunge on the *Tarantula*.

Munitia marched Grant to the stern of the *Tarantula*'s
lower deck and made him kneel at the railing. Pressing the

barrel of her revolver against the base of Grant's skull, she thumbed back the hammer. "*Au revoir*," she said gently.

"Holy moley!" said Grant.

Munitia looked up, and started to scream.

The propeller of the crashing flying machine took her full in the chest. Her pistol went off by dead-hand reflex, but the shot was wildly unaimed and accomplished nothing. Munitia—or at least those larger chunks of her that were still recognizable as human—was flung off the deck and plummeted to the ground, six stories below.

Loveless heard the crash, but was not in a position to see what happened. Frantically, he grabbed the speaking tube. "Munitia, report to the bridge! *Munitia!*"

West and Gordon extricated themselves from the wreckage of the flying machine, then picked up Grant from where he had flattened himself facedown on the deck. "Sorry about that, sir," Gordon said. "Nose up, flaps down. Have to remember that next time."

"Son," Grant said as he dusted himself off, "never apologize for saving a president's life."

West looked at the pile of smoldering wreckage they had just somehow survived coming down in and asked Gordon, "You really want to fly again?"

"Well soon you can *all* fly!" Amazonia growled behind them. "This time with little white angel wings!" West, Gordon, and Grant spun around.

Amazonia and Lippenreider stood there, covering them

with a matched pair of sawed-off shotguns. Amazonia, in particular, was beet red and fairly quivering with rage.

The fires were all out; the *Tarantula* was under control again and steaming steadily south. West, Gordon, and Grant were back in Loveless's power again, and standing on the flying bridge, while Amazonia covered them with a shotgun.

(West nudged Gordon. "How we doing?")

(Gordon frowned. "Same as always.")

("That bad, huh?")

Loveless finished drinking in the cool night air and turned away from the forward rail. "Gentlemen," he began.

He reconsidered, and smiled as he shook his head. "Boys, boys. West and Gordon. If only the considerable effort and ingenuity you have expended in trying to thwart me had been redirected to my cause instead. Think of it. Together, we could have ruled the world!"

West fixed Loveless with a steely glare. "Yeah, well, tell you what. Let me tell you about *my* cause, first. Seems that about four years back, some blood-suckin', baby-murderin', lowlife son of a New Orleans whore built a machine and decided to show the Rebs how to do some *serious* killing. And ever since then I have been tracking down the rabid animal responsible for the massacre at New Liberty, and from what I hear, that's *you*. Now, I think it's a great thing that you went and blew your *co-jones* off and all, and if I live through this I intend to spend the rest of my life thankin' the Lord that the Loveless family line is wiped out like a worthless breed of dogs, but right at the moment I think it is an *incredible* damn pity that you didn't do a better job of just blowing yourself to little bloody, greasy shreds!"

"Uh, Jim?" Gordon said. "I don't think there's any point in antagonizing him any more than he already—"

Loveless tapped a button on the arm of his wheelchair. The floor dropped open beneath West's feet, and West plummeted fifteen feet to the metal deck below, to land with an *oof!* and a sickening thud.

"Lippenreider," Loveless said in a flat voice, "take the helm and keep us on course. Amazonia, let Grant and Gordon watch, but if they try to interfere, blow their brains out." He leaned over and peered through the trapdoor.

"We may not have a woodshed on the *Tarantula*, but that boy is in for a *whuppin'*!"

As Loveless rolled down the ramp onto the lower deck, West staggered uncertainly to his feet. "Very frightening," West said. "Crazy cripple in a wheelchair and all." He circled warily. "Normally I'd think that kicking your ass up around your neck would be too cruel, but in this case, I think it's definitely worth doin'. Bring it on, fool." West touched a finger to his lips, as if embarrassed. "Oops, I forgot. You don't *have* an ass, do you?"

Loveless merely rolled to a stop, and considered West with a strange, faraway smile. Then he pressed a button.

Something kicked in with a low hum and a whine, and the chair started changing. Loveless seemed to grow taller, as the wheels retracted, and the armrests folded in and embraced his lower body. Gears clicked and turned; pneumatic couplings hissed and split apart; and a flywheel whined up to speed. Four complex and spidery mechanical legs, smaller replicas of the units on the *Tarantula*, unfolded from underneath Loveless's body.

With a final metallic click the transformation was complete, and the hybrid human/mechanical *thing* that was Arliss Loveless stepped free of the skeletal remainder of the wheelchair chassis, and towered a good head taller than James West.

"Me and my big mouth," West muttered.

Loveless started rolling up his sleeves and flexing his fists. "Was it someone particularly close to you," he asked, "who perished in the military action at New Liberty?" He took a step closer, moving with an easy, oiled grace.

West fired off a roundhouse kick at Loveless's head. Loveless ducked the blow barely in time.

"Well," Loveless mused, "that certainly seems to have hit a nerve." He feinted with a fist and followed with a lightning flash of a pivot kick that caught West hard in the ribs and sent him flying and rolling across the metal deck.

Loveless pursued. "Your mother, perhaps? Your father, maybe? Do you even know who your father *is*, boy?"

West shook himself out of it and tried to get up off the floor. A cleated metal foot slammed down on his hand and pinned it to the deck, like a butterfly in a collection. West screamed in pain.

Gordon, looking down from the trapdoor on the bridge,

tried to move toward the ramp. Amazonia shoved a gun in his face, and Gordon stepped back.

Loveless released West's hand. "I suppose you thought I'd be slow and clumsy. I imagine you expected these to be mere artificial limbs, like iron hooks and wooden legs." He struck a sudden dramatic pose, with his hands on his hips, then began to dance a hammering metallic flamenco, his pistonlike legs barely missing West's head. "Only now, at the end, do you appreciate the full power of *mechinology.*" He began to clap, shout, and caper like a mad jackhammer. "*And it feels so good to stretch my legs!*" He stopped dancing and grinned.

West suddenly flipped over and threw his legs around in a scissors move, attempting desperately to trip Loveless and take him down. Human shin met alloy strut with a painful clang.

"Ow!" West yelped.

Loveless laughed, and booted West like a soccer ball. West slammed into the railing and felt a rib crack. Loveless stomped over and kicked him again. And again. And *again.* Dragging him away from the railing, Loveless began to kick him back and forth from foot to foot, keeping him in the air for a half dozen blows.

West landed hard on the deck, gasping for breath. His ribs felt like they were alive and moving of their own volition.

Loveless stepped back for a few seconds to admire his footwork, then clomped forward and rested a metal foot on West's head. Slowly, relishing every excruciating moment of it, he began to increase the pressure. "I am gonna pop your head like a grape, boy," he said. Then in a wildly off-key singing voice, he crowed, *"Oh I likes to beat my feets on the Mississippi mud!"*

Gordon turned to Amazonia and Lippenreider and threw his arms wide, beseechingly. "For God's sake, stop this!"

The women didn't even notice that he was talking to them. They were watching Loveless crush West's skull and practically salivating at the prospect of seeing fresh blood and brains.

Unfortunately for the women, they also failed to notice that when Gordon threw his arms wide, the spring-loaded gizmos up his sleeves deposited a notepad into one hand and a loaded derringer in the other.

Gordon had forgotten about the derringer. At the moment, though, it seemed considerably more useful than the pen. He pressed the cold barrel of the gun against Lippenreider's neck. Abruptly she realized that something was wrong and stiffened.

"Drop the guns," Gordon growled.

Lippenreider and Amazonia obediently dropped their guns over the railing, to clatter to the desert below. While Gordon was reconsidering and thinking that maybe he should have said *Hand me the guns, slowly,* Amazonia made eye contact with Lippenreider, and silently mouthed a plan.

"Los!" Amazonia charged Gordon while Lippenreider dodged aside. Instead of wrestling her for the derringer as she expected, though, Gordon dropped back, feinted, and greeted Amazonia's attack with a peculiar little twist and

spin that sent her flying hard against the railing. She hung there for a moment, wide-eyed, terrified, caught in the balance between life and death—

Grant gave her a good hard kick in the seat of the pants, to send her over the railing and chalk one up for Death.

Lippenreider watched Amazonia disappear over the railing and attacked like a screaming harpy. She clawed, she shrieked, she tried to rake Gordon's eyes out—

She went over the railing, too, to plummet six stories to the rocky desert floor, and her death. "*Auf wiedersehen*," Gordon said gently, as he waved good-bye.

The forager ants, brine flies, and buzzards would be happy for *days*.

West's eyes were practically popping out of his head, under the pressure of Loveless's metal leg. Loveless readied himself for one final push, then paused, to reconsider. One quick stomp; one messy smear; where was the fun in *that*? But if he could keep West alive and spend *weeks* killing him, a little at a time . . .

Loveless didn't notice Gordon coming down the ramp from the flying bridge until he heard the man's voice behind him.

"Dr. Loveless! Release West now or I will shoot you!"

Loveless turned to see Gordon, and the Derringer he held. Loveless laughed mirthlessly. "What, you expect to kill me with that pathetic little peashooter?"

Gordon nodded dourly. "If I have to, yes."

Loveless made up his mind on this whole kill 'em now/kill 'em later issue, and decided it was probably best to reach final closure quickly. He grinned. "Why is it, then, that I am unafraid?" He chuckled. "I believe that you gentlemen are the polar opposites of a moral dilemma, and I'm stuck in the middle. On the one hand we have Captain West, a man of primitive vigors, uncomplicated by intellect. On the other, we have Mr. Gordon, a man of ideas, but unlike myself, a man who lacks the *passion* to kill for them. He would like to be able to act his way out of trouble—and for some reason, whenever he's acting, people tend to get killed." Loveless turned to West again and twisted his foot as if grinding out a cigarette.

"Which is why you'd better take your best shot right now, Gordon. Because first I'm going to squash West's head like a rotten watermelon, and then I'm going to kick your guts out and use 'em for a garden hose!" He started to put the final, killing pressure on West.

Gordon used both hands and took careful, steady, aim. "I swear I'll do it," he warned Loveless.

West screamed in pain. "Stop warning him and *do* it!"

"I swear I will!"

Loveless laughed.

Gordon fired. *POP!*

"That was a *gun?*" West moaned.

Loveless seemed nonplussed for a moment, then began to laugh when he realized he was unhurt. "And after all that moral anguish, you missed!"

Gordon shook his head. "I wasn't aiming for you." He gestured down at Loveless's legs, to a metal tube that a minute before was bringing hydraulic fluid to the foot resting on West's head. The severed tube was squirting a thick spurting stream of red oil all over the deck.

Loveless tried to finish West, and found that the leg was now paralyzed. West squeezed out from under the foot, stood up, and began rubbing his neck to get circulation back into it. He nodded at Gordon's Derringer. "The pen is mightier than the sword, huh?"

Gordon nodded sagely. "But some days the sword is a heck of a lot more useful."

Loveless started to back away from West and Gordon, dragging his one useless leg. West cracked his knuckles, set his jaw, and moved in. "And now," he said, "you are gonna pay for that Mississippi crack, you ugly little sawed-off excuse for a man." West raised his fists—

"GORDON!" Grant called out, through the trapdoor from the flying bridge. "Get up here! We've got thirty seconds to stop this thing!" Gordon glanced at West to make sure he had the Loveless situation under control, then dashed up the ramp.

Grant was trying to make sense of the *Tarantula*'s controls when Gordon joined him. "What's the problem, sir?"

In reply, Grant only pointed straight ahead. Two hundred yards off, the flat mesa they were traveling came to a sudden end in a spectacular and probably very scenic cliff.

Gordon's eyes went wide. "Oh."

"Now, Gordon," Grant said, "I guess we'll find out if you're as clever as we all hope you are."

Gordon tried to keep calm, and looked over the myriad of buttons and levers, hoping that Loveless had thought to mark them clearly and in English. When that hope proved fruitless, he pulled one lever just to get his feet wet, and thirty tons of metal spider bucked like a skittish horse. He tried another, and was rewarded by the thing speeding up.

The fight belowdecks was still undecided. West had gotten a few good licks in, but the upper half of Loveless was still a decent boxer and his lower half made him almost impossible to knock over. The battle ranged well aft, then forward again. Suddenly Loveless staggered and grabbed on to the chassis of his wheelchair to keep from falling.

"Had enough?" West sneered.

"Of you," Loveless answered, as he fumbled for a hidden button. West dived to the side, narrowly missed by the buckshot shell concealed in the armrest tube.

With only one shot left, Loveless was not about to risk missing again. Dragging his useless leg, he pushed the chair frame closer to West—

Gordon was starting to panic. Two levers and a button; no good. One lever and two buttons; no good. For a moment he wondered why the machine didn't have a simple and obvious brake pedal, then realized the answer to that question was also simple and obvious. In utter desperation, he pulled two levers back while Grant pushed two other levers forward —

The legs locked up as if the *Tarantula* had suddenly had a fatal heart attack, and the machine came to a grinding stop, teetering on the very edge of the cliff.

At first the only sound Gordon could hear was his own pulse, pounding in his ears. Then, with a slow and terrible groaning like a giant rusty iron hinge, the *Tarantula* began to tip forward. . . .

Loveless's world was focused down to one idea: *KILL WEST.* Nothing else mattered. Nothing else would ever matter. He didn't even care if he himself might die a minute later; all that Dr. Arliss Loveless was or ever would be was concentrated in one vision: Jim West, bleeding, broken, and dead at his feet. If he could just achieve that one little thing, he could die a happy man.

And now, it did seem truly possible. He appeared to have West cornered, as he carefully moved in for the kill. West seemed to be running out of tricks, and the thrashing Loveless had administered earlier was telling. Even when West launched one last attack, it seemed laughably feeble. Graceful, yes; and the flying kick in Loveless's steel plated chest might have seriously hurt a mere human. But Loveless only lost his grip on the chair briefly and staggered back a pace or two.

That's when he noticed that the deck was beginning to tilt. West darted past Loveless and wrapped his arm around the forward railing. Loveless took a step toward him—

And slipped. Puzzled, Loveless looked down and noticed that he was standing in a puddle of hydraulic fluid and that his metal feet had no traction. He tried another step. He slipped again.

"Oh, my God . . ."

The deck continued to tilt forward, like a giant seesaw. Slowly, inexorably, the full terror of what was happening sank into Loveless's mind. He scrabbled. He gasped a little, but was too scared to scream. His metal feet clawed at the oily, tilting deck with total horrible futility. He began sliding toward the forward railing, faster, *faster.* The pitch of the deck increased sharply as the *Tarantula* continued to topple. The dark and jagged canyon below yawned like the hungry mouth of Hell.

"Y'know, Arliss," West said calmly. "It looks like I'm finally gonna be able to put the war behind me. I think you should, too."

Loveless hit the forward railing at considerable velocity. He flipped over it like a tenpin and plunged into the abyss, screaming and tumbling all the way down.

Loveless's departure turned out to be precisely the adjustment the *Tarantula* needed. The machine slowly teetered back from the brink, and Grant and Gordon came belowdecks. "Heavy little bastard, wasn't he?" Gordon said. Grant, Gordon, and West slowly and gingerly clambered down the aft leg and made their way to terra firma. West was the last one to step off, and his 165 pounds were just enough to tip the scales the other way. With a terrible metallic screech, the machine toppled over the edge of the cliff. When it hit bottom the boilers exploded in a fantastic pillar of steam, providing Dr. Arliss Loveless, at least temporarily, with the biggest headstone the West had ever seen.

CHAPTER EIGHTEEN

May 10, 1869: The sun blazed down without mercy, but a light wind arose in the late morning and kept the brine flies off. The Union Pacific and Central Pacific crews had worked overtime to haul away the wreckage and repair the damaged track, and two shiny new locomotives, the 119 and the *Jupiter*, were brought up for the ceremony. President Grant spoke his piece, took off his jacket, and rolled up his sleeves, and with Leland Stanford standing well off to the side, took a mighty overhand swing and drove in the last spike. Hats were tossed in the air, flash powder puffed as photos were taken, and hearty handshakes all around were the order of the day.

As the official ceremony gave way to a general construction-worker kind of party, Grant slipped away and found West and Gordon off to one side. "Gentlemen," Grant said, "I now strongly believe that the United

States is going to be truly *united*. Not because of this simple railroad . . ."

He paused, to scan the crowd. Everywhere Grant looked, there seemed to be bluebloods and immigrants, Indians and Chinese, white and black and every color under the rainbow, all shaking hands and congratulating each other on a job well-done.

". . . but because of you two. And so, while your chests are all puffed out with pride . . ."

Grant reached into his coat pocket, and produced two simple, silver, shield-shaped badges.

"It's clear to me now, the United States needs a permanent Secret Service. Especially now that I've fired those damn Pinkertons." He nodded sidelong at the Pinkerton agents. The Buenaventura cavalry seemed to be taking a certain amount of pleasure in keeping the Pinkertons from boarding the presidential train. Instead, each agent was being handed the reins to a sorry-looking nag.

"Therefore, I have signed into law the creation of an agency whose sole duty is to protect the president and the country from lunatics like Loveless." Grant pinned the badges on West and Gordon's vests.

"Welcome to the Secret Service, Agents Number 1 and 2!" The president shook both their hands.

West fought the urge to look down. "Uh, just out of curiosity, sir, which one of us is Agent Number 1?"

Grant just shook his head, clapped them both on the back, and walked away, chortling.

*   *   *

Rita approached from a crowd of scientists. She was looking extraordinarily fetching, now that she'd finally had a chance to wash up and switch to a print dress and parasol.

"Jim? Arte?"

West and Gordon perked up like a pair of dogs observing the arrival of a nice package of pork chops.

West smiled, and kissed her hand. "Rita, you look great!"

Gordon bowed deeply. "Ravishing. A vision!"

Rita hugged West, then Gordon.

"I just wanted to say thank you for everything you've done for me, before I go back home to Texas."

West frowned. "Texas? Why go back there? Why not come back with me to Washington?"

Gordon elbowed West aside. "Or better still, come with me to Washington. I could introduce you to people I still know in the theater."

West nudged Gordon in the ribs. "She's not really an entertainer, remember?" Gordon glared at West.

Rita interrupted. "Actually, I can't go with either of you." She looked from one suddenly crestfallen hero to the other. "It's not that you aren't both very attractive." She favored Gordon with a smile. "Arte, you're so sophisticated, and such a wonderful cook." She turned to West. "And Jim, you're so brave, and heroic, and you have such great . . . legs.

"And the both of you are so noble, in your own ways. But . . . you see, I'm afraid that I haven't been completely honest with you."

West and Gordon looked at each other. "Uh-oh."

"Professor Escobar is not my father. He's my *husband*." She gestured at the handsome Latino man standing at the edge of the group of scientists, who was clearly waiting for her. Cleaned up, with his hair and goatee neatly trimmed, Professor Escobar was clearly a very handsome and *young* man.

West looked at Escobar again, then at Rita. "Just one question. Why didn't you tell us that in the first place?"

The dark-eyed beauty smiled. "Well, I kept meaning to. But answer honestly, would you *really* have brought me along if you'd known I was married?"

Neither West nor Gordon knew quite how to answer that.

"I didn't think so," Rita said. She turned and walked toward her husband. Then she stopped and smiled back over her shoulder at them. "But at least you still have each other."

West and Gordon stood a long time in silence after Rita left them. At last, West turned to Gordon. "You know something, Arte?" he asked.

"What's that, James?" Gordon answered.

"She's right. Besides, there are a lot of other beautiful women in the world."

Gordon spared one last wistful look in the direction Rita had gone, then turned and started for the *Wanderer*. "That's easy for you to say." Gordon sighed.

"She didn't walk off wearing your best dress."

Also by Bruce Bethke
and available from Warner Aspect

HEADCRASH

Winner of the Philip K. Dick Award

"Laugh-out-loud funny . . . marks Bethke as a formidable satirist and a distinctive new voice."
—*San Francisco Sunday Examiner & Chronicle*

Roadkill on the Information Superhighway. . . Everyone, everywhere, is on-line, and in a world gone PC-haywire, any group can get into your home over the net. The Rodents' Rights Association bombs you with their campaign to stop violence against Semiaquatic Rodent-Americans. . . . The Portly Persons' Liberation Front crusades for radical door enlargement. But not everyone is who they seem. Not even those you trust the most.

"Bethke has taken the computer industry and thrown it in the blender . . . savagely funny."
—*Seattle Weekly*

"A must-read . . . I fell off the couch because I was laughing so loud."
—*St. Paul Pioneer Press*

1113